THE
LAWMAN

A NOVEL

G. MICHAEL HOPF

DEDICATION

TO MY BROTHER JOHN

"Never run a bluff with a six gun."

- Bat Masterson

PROLOGUE

OCTOBER 17, 1865

NEW YORK, NEW YORK

A cold wind from the north swept over Isaac Grant, chilling him to the bone. He stamped his feet against the hard frozen ground with hopes he'd get his blood moving.

It was still fall, yet a frigid cold snap had settled over the city, bringing with it freezing temperatures and causing many to worry that winter was coming early.

Though the war had ended months ago, many resources were being diverted south to help with reconstruction; this included much-needed coal to those rebelling states that had for so long been without. This, however, left a shortage in the northern states. With the shortage driving up prices and the threat of an early and harsh winter, many at Tammany Hall were concerned that the city could be thrust into a state of unrest if they couldn't find a way to remedy the issue. Most houses and tenement buildings were outfitted with coal stoves, the days of wood burning in the city were long gone except for those wealthy who still had them in certain rooms and living spaces. Steam heat was also becoming popular; however, coal was needed to generate the steam in boilers located in basements.

The affairs of such things didn't weigh on Isaac; no,

his mind was on Lucy and the small box he'd been fidgeting with in his right coat pocket. He'd sent her a letter the morning before with instructions to meet him at Mariners Gate on Eighty-Fifth Street at six o'clock. As was normal for him, he arrived early.

Back and forth he paced, not just due to the cold but mainly because he was nervous. He was a man who had seen many things, including honorable service in the war as an officer in the Sixty-Seventh New York Volunteer Regiment. He'd seen his share of campaigns and combat, yet here he was on the cusp of something that vexed him like no other.

Anxious as to where she might be, he removed his pocket watch and opened it. Seeing it was five minutes past six, he grunted, "Where are you, Lucy?" He pocketed his watch and looked all around, hoping he'd see her smiling face coming his way. As the minutes passed, his anxiety turned to frustration. Questions quickly popped into his head. Had she not gotten the letter? Had her father, a man who made it abundantly clear that Isaac's affections weren't welcome, prevented her from coming? Or worse, did she choose of her own volition not to come?

Once more he pulled out his watch to check the time.

"Isaac!" a voice cried out from across the street.

He craned his head in the direction of the familiar voice and spotted Lucy waving. Seeing her brought a smile to his chilled face.

Lucy scurried across the street as fast as she could

considering she was wearing a heavy dress and covered up with a thick winter coat. "I'm so sorry I'm late, my dear," she said, embracing him warmly.

As her arms wrapped around him, his angst melted away. "It's fine. I'm just happy to see you."

"When I received the letter simply telling me to be here, I so wanted to know why. Are you well? Do you have news to tell me? Is it about the job with the law firm?" she asked, peppering him with questions.

Isaac had studied law in Albany and was hoping to find a position in New York at any firm that would take him, but each opportunity he presented himself to, he found obstacles. What he hadn't counted on was the headwinds created by the elite class, who looked down on a middle-class man such as Isaac, who came from a fairly well-to-do family. His father hadn't been rich but had created a business and fought to get his family status and his son an education.

"Shall we take a walk?" he asked, holding his arm out.

"Let's," she said with a sweet smile as she took his arm.

They entered the park, slowly walking along one of the many paths there.

"I want to thank you for coming out. I know it wasn't easy for you, considering your father," Isaac said.

"I pray you will forgive me," she said.

"Forgive you for what?" he asked, confused by her statement.

"I wasn't truthful to my father. I hope you don't

think I often lie or misrepresent myself."

"Heavens no, I know your father, and let me preface what I'm about to say with the fact that I do believe he's a great man, but we both know he doesn't hold me in high regard, so I expected you would have to…"

"Lie?" She chuckled.

"I didn't want to say that word, but yes, lie," he said, laughing.

Tugging on his arm with excitement, she said, "So tell me."

"Tell you?"

She gave him an awkward look and asked, "Did you forget why you asked me to come here?"

"Oh no, not at all," he said.

"Then tell me," she pressed.

"Lucy, as you know, I've been through a lot in my life. After graduation I expected to work for a law firm in Albany near my family; then the war began. Like any man, I did my duty and volunteered. At the time I thought the war had upended my life, and may even kill me; yet I survived, and out of the horrors of it all, I found you. Can you imagine that? How can fate be so gracious? It was as if it was fate all along. I may not have ever found you had those rebels not seceded, forcing us to stop them."

"Are you saying you're grateful for the rebels?"

"In a way, yes, I am," he replied. He collected his thoughts and continued, "Just when I imagined my life was going off course, you stepped in front of me at the hospital. I know many men tried to woo you, but you stood firm in your convictions and true to yourself. When

I asked you if we could correspond, you said yes. Let me say that day is one of my fondest to remember."

Stopping him, she stepped in front of him and took his gloved hands. "Isaac Grant, what are you doing?"

Looking deeply into her green eyes, he answered, "Lucy Mae Wagner, I stand here in awe of you." He cleared his throat and dropped to one knee. Removing the box from his coat pocket, he opened it to reveal a small ring with a sapphire stone. Holding it up, he said, "I cannot imagine my life without you. Will you do me the honor of being my wife?"

In shock she covered her mouth. Tears streamed down her chilled cheeks. Looking at the ring, she gushed, "It's so beautiful."

"It was my grandmother's. My mother had it shipped to me. I promise when I get a position and start making money, I'll get you your own."

"Oh no, no, this is perfect. It's so lovely," she said, pinching the ring with her fingers and laying it on her open palm.

"Is that a yes?" he asked.

Wiping her cheeks, she replied, "Yes."

He jumped to his feet, removed the glove from her left hand, and placed the ring on her finger. "It fits perfectly."

"It does," she said as more tears appeared.

"I love you, Lucy," he said, leaning in to give her a kiss.

"I love you too," she said.

They kissed and embraced with passersby smiling

and giving their congratulations.

"I need to meet with your father soon and ask him for your hand," Isaac said.

"Oh, how I want to be a fly on the wall for that conversation." She laughed.

"I know he'll disapprove at first, but I'll win him over, I swear," he said confidently.

"Father's just getting over how the war turned out," Lucy said, referring to her father's deep ties to a group of anti-war democrats known as the Copperheads.

"He must see now how what we did was of value. We kept the Union together; that was the most important thing," Isaac said, his tone turning to one of passion. He was a true believer in the cause he'd fought for and would defend it to anyone.

"You know him, he didn't then, nor does he now, see how losing so many men was worth it," she said.

"Well, the war is over; that is the past. We must now look to the future," Isaac happily said.

"Agreed."

"Shall I get you a cup of hot chocolate to celebrate our engagement?" he asked.

"That sounds like the perfect drink for the occasion, especially on an evening as cold as this," she said, smiling sweetly.

He offered his arm, and together they exited the park, headed for the closest café.

OCTOBER 21, 1865
NEW YORK, NEW YORK

The cold snap that was gripping New York hadn't relented, raising tensions all throughout the city as people fought for any piece of coal they could get their hands on.

While the chill was in the air outside, it was even colder inside 12 East Sixty-Ninth Street. There Isaac sat, his hands clasped in his laps as Lucy's father, Everett Wagner, lambasted him.

"Mr. Grant, while I can appreciate what you've accomplished with getting your law degree, but your family—your father merely owns a small mill; he's not known in the circles I frequent. I'd also be remiss if I didn't look at your politics and say that having a man who openly supported a barbaric war that killed hundreds of thousands was not fit to be a part of my family and take my daughter's hand in wedlock!"

"Mr. Wagner, my father is a great man who has worked hard all his life to get what he has. He sacrificed greatly to provide for us and ensure I was given an education. Secondly, I love your daughter and—"

Interrupting Isaac, Everett continued, "Love is not enough; no, it is not. A marriage is a contract in the eyes of God, and I must also look at this coupling socially. How will my friends and colleagues look upon me if I allow a man from an unknown family in Albany to marry my only daughter?"

"You're saying I'm not good enough," Isaac said.

"That is precisely what I'm saying, but I still can't

forget your support for that war. Even God did not approve of that war. Now I've said enough. I think you should leave." He turned and placed his hands on the mantel of the roaring fireplace.

Isaac glared at Everett's rotund frame. A burning rage was building in him, but he kept it at bay. Exploding on Everett and delivering a litany of reasons why his support for the war was just and righteous would not win him over. Biting his tongue, he sat and stared at the floor.

Everett faced Isaac and barked, "Mr. Grant, you are excused. I have nothing further to discuss with you."

From the second-floor landing of the stairs just outside the den, Lucy sat and listened in horror as her father tore into Isaac. Her heart melted as her father pounded away.

Standing tall, Isaac declared, "Mr. Wagner, I love your daughter. While I disagree with much of what you said, I respect you because you're an accomplished man and hold a positive impact in the community; however, I can't leave without addressing some of the mischaracterizations you've said about me."

Upon hearing those words leave Isaac's mouth, Lucy hopped to her feet and raced down the stairs and into the room. "Father, please, I love him. I've loved him since the first day I saw him," she begged as she ran up to Everett and took his hand.

Lowering his tone, he replied, "My darling Lucy, you know my feelings about the war and about his upbringing. Not only did the nation suffer, but our family did as well. Losing Robert will forever haunt me. And while I don't blame Mr. Grant here specifically, I blame those warmongers in the capital and the devilish Mr. Lincoln; thank God he's now gone."

"Mr. Lincoln was a great man!" Isaac blared.

"Mr. Grant, you're not helping yourself here. In fact, I find your tone to be indignant. Do you not know who you're talking to?" Everett barked back.

Walking over to Isaac, Lucy took his hand and said, "My dear, it's time for you to go. Let me walk you to the door."

Not arguing with her, Isaac nodded. He glanced at Everett and said, "I'll return in a week to ask again."

"And my answer will be the same. You should know, Mr. Grant, I'm not a man to be trifled with," Everett shot back. "I'll never consent to this marriage, you hear me? Not even with my dying breath will I ever consent."

"I'll marry your daughter with or without your consent," Isaac fired back, instantly regretting his word choice and tone.

Shooting Isaac a look of disdain, Everett sneered, "That will never happen, I can assure you. Now goodbye, Mr. Grant."

Restraining himself from replying further, Isaac followed Lucy to the front door.

"Sweetheart, if we're to be together, you must show restraint. While I love and adore your passion, it does no good with my father. He feels the way he does and for good cause. Losing my brother in the war has forever haunted him. Now go, I'll work on him some more. Do come in a week's time though and ask again."

"But he's so stubborn," Isaac said.

"He is, but challenging him isn't smart. You must show restraint. My father was right, he's not a man to be trifled with; even Tammany Hall gives him respect. So please, I beg you, don't rile him up again like you've done."

"He just makes me so mad," Isaac confessed.

"I understand, but please promise me you'll keep your tone civil next time," Lucy urged.

"I promise," he said.

"You won't go back on it, will you?" she asked.

"No, I won't." He sighed. "Gerald gave me the same advice you are. He said don't go in there on your high horse."

"Maybe you should listen to your friend," Lucy said.

Gerald was an old childhood friend of Isaac's who now lived in New York City. He hadn't gone to war like Isaac due to a physical ailment but instead made his way to the city and had begun working in the shipyards. After the war, the two had reconnected and would often see each other.

"Can I see you sooner than next week?" Isaac asked.

"Of course, come for lunch in three days' time," she replied. "But promise me if you see my father, you'll be respectful."

Isaac kissed her hand and said, "I love you and I promise."

"I love you too. Now go before my father has you arrested."

"For what, loving his daughter?" Isaac laughed.

"I'm not making light of it. He knows many people; my father is a powerful man, you know this. Please be mindful next time," Lucy said. Touching Isaac's face tenderly, she continued, "Till we see each other again."

"Till then," Isaac said, leaving the warmth of the house and heading into the cold dark night.

***

Isaac replayed the encounter with Mr. Wagner over and over in his mind, regretting some of the things he'd said and internally praising others. It was an exercise he'd commit to for the week so that during his next attempt, he'd be more polished.

Screams and commotion down the street tore him away from his thoughts. He looked but couldn't make out what was happening. Curious, he approached to discover a large group of men robbing a lumber and hardware store.

Having seen so much horror during the war, he wasn't the least bit fazed by robbery; in fact, he found it somewhat entertaining to watch as men ran in and out, many taking with them sacks of coal and other items of value.

A boy jumped from the shattered front window and tripped on the ground, his face skidding across the sidewalk littered with shards of glass. Yelping in pain, the boy cried out.

Seeing the boy was bleeding badly, Isaac walked up to him and knelt down. "You're hurt."

"I cut myself real bad," the boy cried.

He was younger than Isaac first thought. Seeing him up close, Isaac realized he couldn't have been older than seven. Taking a handkerchief from his pocket, he placed it against the deep cut on the boy's face. "Press this against the cut."

The boy did as he said.

"Say, what are you doing?" a gruff man barked from the shadows.

Isaac looked up to see a man coming at him, his fists clenched.

"The boy is hurt. I was merely—" Isaac said as he went to stand.

The man said nothing else. He cocked his right arm back and punched Isaac squarely in the face.

Isaac reeled from the blow, falling and hitting his head hard against a light post. He looked up and saw the man wasn't satisfied with the first strike.

He came down on Isaac with what felt like an endless barrage of punches.

Isaac unsuccessfully tried to defend himself, but the first blow had left him dazed and incapable of fighting back.

Taking Isaac by his coat, the man lifted him up, cocked his arm back, and said, "This will teach you." The man delivered the punch, hitting Isaac on the jaw and knocking him out.

OCTOBER 22, 1865
NEW YORK, NEW YORK

Isaac woke to the vilest stench. He went to sit up, but his body reminded him of the beating he'd received hours before. Looking around the dimly lit space, he made out vertical bars on the far wall. Squinting to focus, he then realized he was in jail. Aware of his predicament, he sprang to his feet and hobbled to the door. "Is anyone there?"

A raspy voice from the adjacent cell barked, "Shut up."

"Where am I?" Isaac cried out.

"You're in hell. Now shut up!" the voice shot back.

A door creaked open, letting in precious light. In came a burly man dressed in a blue uniform. He headed directly for Isaac's cell. Stopping just beyond arm's reach, he said, "Are you Mr. Grant?"

"I am, yes, I'm Mr. Grant." Isaac sighed with relief, believing he was being released.

"Step away from the door," the man said.

Isaac did as he said.

The man unlocked the cell door and opened it wide. "Step out."

Again, Isaac did as he requested without protest.

Using a rusty pair of shackles, the man secured Isaac's arms in front of him and escorted him out of the darkened jailhouse and into a courtroom nearby. "Where am I going?"

"To see the judge," the man replied.

"Judge? For what? I've done nothing wrong. I was attacked. You should be finding the man who assaulted me," Isaac said, confused by what was happening. Inside the small courtroom, Isaac scanned the space to find it was empty save for one familiar face, Mr. Everett Wagner. "You're a sight for sore eyes, Mr. Wagner. I'm so happy to see you."

The man took Isaac and sat him behind a table.

Isaac quickly turned around and said, "Mr. Wagner, what is going on? Are you here to get me out?"

Everett ignored Isaac.

"Mr. Wagner?" Isaac asked, concerned by Everett's silence.

A door opened and closed towards the front of the courtroom. A man dressed in a black robe came in and took the seat at the bench. He examined a piece of paper then looked up. "Why is the accused not standing?"

The man came up and lifted Isaac to his feet.

Knowing the decorum of a courtroom, Isaac said, "Your Honor, I respectfully—"

"Silence, you were not summoned to speak," the judge said. He looked past Isaac and saw Mr. Wagner. "Nice to see you."

Baffled by what was happening, Isaac couldn't restrain himself. "Your Honor, there must be a mistake."

Looking up again, the judge replied, "Since the accused won't remain silent and allow me the time to review the statements, I'll begin. Mr. Isaac Grant, you've been charged with robbery, breaking and entering, theft, and inciting a riot."

"Inciting a riot?" Isaac asked.

The judge hammered the gavel and barked, "Will the accused remain silent until I call on him!"

Isaac shook his head in disbelief.

"How do you plead?" the judge asked.

"Not guilty on all charges," Isaac said. "If you're referring to the break-in, I witnessed it and—"

"Will the witness come forward," the judge said.

Looking around as to who that might be, Isaac watched in shock as Everett walked up and stood before the judge.

"What do you know about the charges against Mr. Grant?" the judge asked.

"Aren't you going to swear him in?" Isaac asked.

Slamming the gavel down hard, the judge barked, "Will the bailiff restrain and gag the accused until I need him to speak."

The man stepped up behind Isaac and secured a thick leather strap around Isaac's mouth.

"Last I saw of Mr. Grant, he was angry—left my house in a blind fury, to be more exact. If you're asking me if he could commit such a crime, I have to say...yes, he could," Everett lied. "In fact, I knew he had been consorting with some rough individuals for some time, but we thought he could move past his ways. Unfortunately, he wasn't able to."

Isaac leapt to his feet and began to yell from behind his gag.

"Bailiff, secure the accused," the judge ordered. Putting his attention back on Everett, he said, "You're an upstanding and respected pillar of our community, and what you say holds water with this court. Thank you, you may be seated."

Everett walked back to his seat, not giving Isaac even a glance.

"Will the next witness please come in," the judge said.

A guard opened the door and escorted in an unfamiliar man. He walked up to the bench and stood.

"Are you Frank Sellers?" the judge asked.

"Yes."

"Do you know the accused sitting behind you?" the judge asked.

Frank glanced back for a second before facing the judge again. "That's him, he planned the robbery. I was there when he did it."

Isaac leapt to his feet and grunted.

"Secure the accused!" the judge barked, slamming down his gavel.

Two other men, guards, entered the courtroom. They rushed to Isaac and held him down.

"If the accused acts out one more time, I'll add contempt of court to the charges," the judge howled. Looking back to Frank, he continued. "So you know the accused?"

"Yes."

"And you know of his plan to rob that establishment last night?"

"Yes. He planned it. He's the ringleader," Frank said, nodding his head vigorously.

"Thank you, you may leave," the judge said.

Frank turned and rushed out of the courtroom.

The judge removed a small pair of glasses from the bridge of his nose and placed them on the bench in front of him. He looked at Isaac and said, "I have considered all the evidence and now the eyewitness testimony that corroborates and supports what occurred last night. This leads me to conclude that you're guilty on all counts. Mr. Grant, you will be sent to and housed in Blackwell's Island Penitentiary for a period of no less than twenty years. I pray you will use this time to reflect on what you've done." The judge slammed the gavel down, got up, and exited the room.

Horrified by the nightmare scenario that had just played out before him, Isaac squirmed and hollered behind his gag, frantic to get free.

Everett stood and walked up to a mortified Isaac, leaned in, and with a devilish grin on his face said, "I told you that you'll never marry my Lucy. You should have listened to me, but you didn't. This is what hubris brings. Enjoy your time on the island."

Isaac lashed out but was quickly subdued by the bailiff and the two guards.

Unable to control Isaac in his current state, the bailiff took a small club from his belt and struck Isaac over the head, knocking him out.

Everett strolled out of the courtroom, his face showing the pleasure he was taking in the moment.

The three men picked Isaac up and hauled him away.

CHAPTER ONE

OCTOBER 21, 1869

BLACKWELL'S ISLAND PENITENTIARY, NEW YORK CITY, NEW YORK

The first year he spent on Blackwell's Island, Isaac wrote letters to city councilmen, senators and congressional leaders, detailing the miscarriage of justice he'd been a victim of, yet he never received a reply. It seemed that he'd been locked away and left to rot. When the first year turned to the second, with no replies or visits except from his best friend, Gerald, he began to worry that he would be forced to suffer another nineteen years for a crime he didn't commit.

By year three, all hope had left him, and he now was resigned to his condition and tried to make the best of it.

Then year four came, and even Gerald stopped visiting. His resignation now became despair. He could no longer imagine living like he was and wanted it all to end. So after much thought, he unsuccessfully tried to kill himself. This only led to worse living conditions, as he was placed in a cell by himself with nothing that could be fashioned to aid him in committing suicide.

Stuck in solitary confinement with only rotting and moldy straw for a bed, he lay pondering just how he could end his miserable life.

The distinct sound of a guard holding keys came

from the other side of his door.

The door unlocked and opened. A tall and slim man wearing a blue guard uniform stepped inside his cell and tossed his clothes at him. "Put them on and be quick about it."

Isaac stared at the clothes. They were his from that very night four years before.

The guard looked nervous. He peeked through the door then back to Isaac. "Hurry if you want to leave."

Sitting up, Isaac asked, "Leave? Go where?"

The guard stepped forward and whispered, "If you want to get out of here, now's your chance, but you must hurry."

A perplexed grimace took over Isaac's face. "I don't understand."

"Your friend Gerald sends his regards and has secured your unofficial release. Now hurry," the guard said.

Unsure if this was a ruse of some sort, Isaac moved slowly.

The guard took Isaac firmly by his arm and lifted him to his feet. "If you're not dressed in five minutes and out that door, your chance to leave this place is over."

He still had sixteen years left of his sentence. If this was a ruse and he was captured trying to make a daring escape, what was the worst that could happen? His life was essentially over if he stayed. Jumping to his feet, he ripped off the ratty clothing he had on and swiftly put on his old clothes.

Once Isaac was dressed, the guard escorted him out

of the cell and down the darkened and wet hallway until he reached a large metal door. He removed a set of keys and fiddled through them until he found the one he wanted. He inserted it into the lock and turned it until he heard a loud clack. He swung the door open and glanced at Isaac. "Now go. Run."

"Where?" Isaac asked, looking out through the door into the pitch black.

"Go down the stairs to the bottom, and go out the door, it will be unlocked. Once outside, head to the south of the island. There's a man with a boat set to meet you."

"Which way is south?" Isaac asked.

"When you go out the door, you'll be facing south; just head in that direction. The man with the boat will be just south of the prison grounds."

"Isn't there a perimeter wall?" Isaac asked.

"Just a six-foot wall, climb it and go south until you reach the riverbank," the guard said.

"And Gerald sent you?" Isaac asked, confused.

"Yes. He said for you to flee the city. Don't come find him," the guard growled. He was growing nervous that the longer this took, the higher the chances were he'd get caught.

Isaac stared into the blackness and, without hesitating one more second, disappeared into it.

CORRIGAN RESIDENCE, BANE, NEVADA

Lucy struggled to wake. Her body felt as if a ton of bricks were lying upon it, keeping her pressed into the mattress.

The light of the early morning sun peeked through the corner of the drawn blinds, illuminating the ornate and beautifully decorated bedroom.

Knowing Mortimer would soon be calling on her, she sluggishly sat up and went for the bottle of laudanum on the nightstand. Taking it and the glass dropper next to it, she opened the bottle and inserted the dropper. Filling the tube, she dropped its contents on her tongue and pressed her mouth closed. She allowed the liquid to sit on her tongue for a count of ten then swallowed. She closed the bottle and placed it back on the nightstand.

Sitting on the edge of the bed, her feet dangling just above the cold wood floor, she stared at the bottle. The opium-based medicine had become an anchor for her, or as she sometimes mentioned, it had become her friend. Ever since arriving in the mining town of Bane nine months before, she had taken to the medicine to relieve the anxiety attacks she'd been having. It had helped by numbing her, but it had also made her dependent to the point she couldn't rise for the day without taking some, nor could she manage to go throughout the day without it.

A tap on the door told her Mortimer, her husband, was home from his early morning meetings. "Yes."

"Are you decent?" Mortimer asked politely.

"Yes, come in," she replied as she got up and made her way to the vanity, which was located against the far wall.

Mortimer entered the room, a smile stretched across his face. "I have some good news. I came home to share it with you." He hustled to a small chair adjacent to the vanity and sat down.

As she ran the hairbrush through her thick brown hair, she said, "Do tell me."

"I think I found the man who will be perfect for the position," he blurted out happily.

"Do you mean for sheriff?" she asked, her speech slurred from the dose of laudanum.

Sensing she was under the influence, he smiled and said, "Yes, for sheriff." Mortimer didn't think much of her using laudanum, as it had been his idea for her to seek medical attention for her anxiety and the migraines she so often complained of having. After having been married for three years, an arranged marriage set up by Lucy's father, he'd seen a shift in her demeanor upon their arrival in Bane. He knew she didn't like it there, but there wasn't any other option. Mortimer was a successful businessman who was fifteen years her senior and had been a partner of her father's in a shipping enterprise. He was always seeking new opportunities, so when he'd heard that a silver-mining town in Nevada was available for purchase, he immediately secured it and took Lucy out west. Bane had since proven to be a savvy business investment and had provided Mortimer with significant profits. The only issue that caused a constant disruption in town was the lack of law and order.

When they had arrived, murders, rapes and assaults were a daily occurrence in the town that boasted seven thousand people, many of whom worked in the mines. Mortimer had strived to get the crime under control by hiring a sheriff and giving him adequate resources to bring on a team of four deputies; however, not two months went by before the first sheriff had been gunned down in the streets.

Mortimer promoted one of the deputies to fill the position. Within weeks, crime and murder within the town limits lowered, but the new sheriff wasn't able to stop the rogue bands of road agents and bandits from robbing incoming shipments and stagecoaches. Pressed by Mortimer to find an answer, the new sheriff promised to crack down. When nothing changed, Mortimer came to discover after conducting an investigation that the new sheriff was being paid off by someone in town who happened to be benefitting from the robberies. Mortimer fired the sheriff and placed an advertisement in many newspapers, looking for a new lawman to come in and handle the situation, and now he believed he had found the right person.

"That's nice," she said.

"His name is Ethan Travis and he hails from San Antonio, Texas. His most recent job was as the chief of police in Scranton, Pennsylvania, but he's most notable for being a Texas Ranger before the war. He'll be perfect for the position," Mortimer said.

"That's nice," she repeated.

Seeing that she wasn't really listening, he sat and looked at her. He loved her dearly, though at times he could sense she didn't love him the same. He strived to do everything he could to make her happy, but she just wasn't. He had thought about hiring a city manager to handle the day-to-day operations of the town and mines but had found in his years of operating other successful businesses that no one could do a better job than the owner and visionary.

She placed the brush down and swiveled in her seat to face him. "I'm happy that we have a new sheriff coming. When will he arrive?"

Happy to see she did have an interest, he answered, "Soon, I expect him to be here in a little over a week. He's tying up loose ends then will take the train out to Elko then coach it from there."

"I know having Mr. Travis will ease your mind," she said.

"It will, and I've made sure to insulate him from the corruption too by paying him twice the salary of any town sheriff, and I plan on offering him bonuses too if he can find the ringleader behind those raids on the shipments," Mortimer said.

"Well, I hope he works out. Losing all those goods isn't good for the townspeople," she said.

"We'll get it figured out; I know, I'm an optimist," he said.

Patting his hand, she said, "That's why my father liked you."

"Speaking of your father, I need to send him a wire and let him know; he's taken great interest in this endeavor of mine out here. I think he might even want to invest."

"You're looking for investors? So his trip out here isn't just social?" she asked.

"It's both. You know your father better than anyone. I do know he does wish to see you more than anything. And to answer your question about investors, I want to expand the operations, and I'll be needing some additional capital for that. So I thought why not keep it in the family?" he said, smiling.

She furrowed her brow and frowned.

"What's the matter?" he asked.

Not wanting to express how she really felt, she lied and said, "My head, it hurts. I think I have a migraine coming on again."

Getting to his feet, he said, "I'll let you get back to getting ready for the day. How about we have lunch together?"

"That sounds nice. Let Phyllis know; tell her I'd like the potato soup," Lucy said.

"I will," Mortimer said, leaning down and kissing Lucy on the right cheek. "I love you."

"And I you," she said, reaching for a makeup brush.

Mortimer left the room, closing the door behind him.

Lucy stared at her reflection in the mirror, her thoughts drifting to Isaac. Four years had passed since she'd last seem him, and still she couldn't fathom he'd actually done what he had been accused of doing. She would often think of what her life would have been if they had been allowed to marry. Would they have had children by now? Would they have lived in New York, or would he have found a job somewhere else, maybe in New England or even in the Midwest? Never seeing him again was what she found so disturbing. He'd left that night after arguing with her father and never returned. It was as if he had died, but she knew he hadn't. She had tried to visit him, but her father had forced her not to. "Where are you, Isaac?" she asked out loud.

NEW YORK, NEW YORK

By the time Isaac reached Lower Manhattan, the sun was rising to the east. He hurried along the streets, looking over his shoulder as he went, fully expecting someone to notice him or to see a squad of police in pursuit. He crisscrossed the narrow streets until he reached the tenement building where Gerald had last lived.

He looked at the door but paused before going in. The last Isaac had seen of his old friend had been two years ago. Not having Lucy come visit was one thing, then having his parents disown him was another, but when Gerald stopped coming, his heart had shattered, as he was now alone in the world with no one he could turn to. After experiencing the ordeal in the courtroom with Everett, he suspected the reason Lucy never came to visit, but there wasn't anything holding Gerald back, he thought. So why did he stop, and then why have him freed suddenly? He had many questions, and in order to get answers, he needed to find his old friend.

He climbed the steep steps of the building and entered. The cries of babies and howls of aggravated parents hit his ears, followed by a stale odor that sent his senses into overload. He immediately darted up the stairs, skipping every other step until he reached the fourth floor. He hurried to Gerald's door, passing several curious people in the hallway, who gave him suspicious looks. Standing at the door, he exhaled deeply then rapped on the door.

A voice called out from inside, but Isaac couldn't make out if it was Gerald.

Straightening out the wrinkles in his stained clothes as best he could, he stood upright, spine stiffened, and waited for whoever he had heard to answer.

The door unlocked and creaked open just a slight bit. A man peeked around the door. "What do you want?"

"Gerald?" Isaac asked.

The man opened the door fully. His eyes were wide with surprise. "Isaac?"

Recognizing his old friend, Isaac replied, "Yes, it's me."

"What are you doing here?" Gerald asked, stepping out of the way and inviting Isaac into his small six-hundred-square-foot apartment with a motion of his hand. "Hurry, get inside."

Isaac stepped across the threshold. He scanned the apartment and instantly took notice that Gerald was apparently living destitute by the amount of garbage and filth that littered the space. "Why?"

Gerald peeked outside to see if anyone was looking but saw the hall was now empty. He closed the door and locked it. Turning around, he scoffed, "What are you doing here?"

"To find answers," Isaac replied.

"I gave specific instructions for you not to come here. You've just escaped prison and now you're here? You should be heading out of the city."

"I need to know why?" Isaac said.

"Why what?"

"Why did you stop seeing me then out of nowhere have me released?" Isaac asked.

Gerald scrunched his face and scurried to the small coal stove in the middle of the room. He opened it and tossed in a couple of pieces of coal, then, using a poker, stirred the fiery contents inside. "Sorry it's so cold in here. I'm a bit short on funds these days," he said, closing the door. He cinched a blanket around his shoulders tighter and said, "It's a long story and one I'd rather not be addressing. You need to leave this apartment and the city immediately."

"No, I need answers."

"Are you cold?" Gerald asked.

"I'm fine. Now please tell me why you had me released?" Isaac said, bringing the conversation back to his recent escape.

"It was the right thing to do," Gerald replied before heading to a tiny table butted up against the wall. "Can I offer you something to eat, a piece of bread maybe?"

"No, Gerald, I don't want anything to eat," Isaac replied.

"Then something to drink? I have some brandy or maybe a glass of port?" Gerald said, snatching two bottles from a shelf and heading back to the main living space, where two chairs sat.

"Why didn't you come back?" Isaac asked point-blank.

Gerald set the bottles down and mumbled something unintelligible.

"Two years," Isaac said, reminding Gerald of the time since he'd last seen him. "I thought the worst had occurred to you, that maybe you'd died."

"Almost died would be the correct thing to say," Gerald said, pouring a glass full of brandy and swigging it. He wiped his mouth using his sleeve and poured another glass full.

"Is that why?" Isaac asked.

Putting the glass to his lips, Gerald answered, "No, that's not why."

"Then tell me; you owe me that much," Isaac said.

Gerald tossed the glass back, turned and replied, "I was told in no uncertain terms not to see you again. And if I did, I could possibly lose my position at the shipyards."

Isaac gritted his teeth and seethed. "It was him, right?"

"I don't know who did what, but when the foreman warned me to stay away from the prison and you, I had to, you must understand," Gerald pleaded, a look of agony written all over his face.

"I understand completely," Isaac said. "But why risk it all to help me escape?"

"Like I said, it was the right thing to do," Gerald answered. He lifted the bottle of brandy and said, "Are you sure you won't take a glass, it's quite good."

Isaac waved off the drink and answered, "Where is she?"

"You won't find her in the city. She's gone," Gerald said.

"Where is she?" Isaac asked.

"I read in the paper…" Gerald said but cut himself short for fear that what he'd say would upset Isaac.

"Go on," Isaac urged.

Taking a seat in one of the chairs, Gerald looked down at the floor and said, "She was married to a man, a businessman who had some affiliation with her father, about a year after you were imprisoned."

"And you chose not to tell me during one of your visits?" Isaac asked angrily.

"I didn't think you needed to hear that. For Christ's sake, Isaac, you were living in hell already; I thought telling you would only make your emotional state worse. I thought the worst, that you might hurt yourself or even, God forbid, kill yourself," Gerald explained.

Isaac instantly thought about the time he had tried to end his own life.

"You look well…enough," Gerald said.

"Why did this happen to me?" Isaac asked himself, his head now buried in his hands.

"You know why," Gerald said.

"I know why, but why would God do this to me? Is he testing me? Why torture me? Have I done something wrong? Do I deserve this?" Isaac said, asking the same questions that he'd asked himself over and over during the last four years.

"I don't think God had anything to do with this; sounds more like the devil, if you ask me," Gerald replied.

"You said she isn't in the city. Where is she?" Isaac asked, lifting his head from his hands and looking directly at Gerald.

"Out west, her husband purchased a silver-mining town. Can you believe that? The man is so rich he bought an entire town."

"Where?" Isaac asked.

"A mining town in Nevada—"

"What's the name of the town?" Isaac asked, interrupting Gerald.

"I can't quite remember," Gerald said.

"Think hard."

"Why? Are you planning to go there? And if so, why would you do that? She's married, Isaac, don't be a fool," Gerald said.

"I need to know. She owes me that," Isaac answered, his tone filled with spite.

"She might owe you, but do you honestly think she'll tell you? Her husband will have you arrested or, worse, killed. He's a rich and powerful man," Gerald blared.

"I don't care, my life is gone. I can no longer practice law, as the state bar has revoked my license. I'm ruined. My parents have disowned me, and for a while I even thought my best friend had given up on me," Isaac said.

"I told you what happened. What would you expect me to do?" Gerald asked.

Looking around the apartment, Isaac asked, "Have you lost your job?"

"No, but the shipyard has cut back my hours. If you haven't heard, we're in an economic recession; things are bad. Some say the economy could collapse," Gerald replied.

"I'm sorry to hear that, and, no, I hadn't heard about what's happening in the country. I didn't get much in the way of news while imprisoned," Isaac said.

"You didn't answer my question," Gerald said, referring to his earlier question about why Isaac would go out west to find Lucy.

"I need to know. I need to see her again, just once more," Isaac said, his tone now shifting to sadness.

"You still love her, don't you?"

"I never stopped though I had some dark moments. I just feel that it was her father; he orchestrated this entire thing all because he didn't want us to marry. He had me put in prison, and if I were a betting man, I'd guess he prevented her from seeing me."

"Or maybe she thought you were a criminal," Gerald said.

"Regardless, there's nothing for me in New York. I want to go out west. There I can start a new life," Isaac said. "And who knows, maybe she still loves me. Maybe we have a chance."

"Don't be a damn fool. You have one thing correct, there's nothing here for you, and there's nothing more I can say that will bring you solace. I need you to leave, not because I want you to go, but because they may find you the longer you linger."

"Now tell me, where is she?" Isaac asked, sensing

that Gerald knew the specific town.

Gerald sighed loudly and said, "A town called Bane. I don't know where it is specifically. All I know is it's a silver-mining town."

"And who is her husband?" Isaac asked.

"A Mr. Mortimer Corrigan, by all accounts I've heard, he's a decent man," Gerald answered.

"Lucy Corrigan, hmm," Isaac mused.

"This is a mistake. I shouldn't have told you anything," Gerald growled.

"I need a horse if I'm to make the journey," Isaac said, ignoring Gerald's last comment.

"You're really going no matter what I say?"

"You've known me your entire life, you know I'm going," Isaac said.

"Then take the train," Gerald said.

"I thought about that, but I'll need a horse once I get to Missouri…"

"Take the Transcontinental Railway, it goes from coast to coast. They've just opened it up," Gerald said, informing Isaac of the monumental transportation achievement.

"There's a train that goes from one side of the country to the other?" Isaac asked.

"Yes, there is; isn't it marvelous?" Gerald said, smiling.

"Where do I catch it?" Isaac asked.

"That I don't know, but I'm sure you can find out easily," Gerald said. "Are you sure this is what you want to do?"

"I've never been surer of myself. I need to go see her; then after, I'll find a new place to live, under an alias. I'll begin anew."

Gerald got to his feet and shuffled to the shelf where he'd gotten the bottles of brandy and port. He took a jar down, opened it, and removed a wad of cash. He turned to Isaac and said, "There's one hundred fifty-five dollars here."

"I can't take your money," Isaac said, waving him off.

"Take it. If you're to take that train, you'll need it, and you'll need to buy a horse once you get there, some new clothes and even a firearm," Gerald said, sticking the cash in Isaac's face.

"I won't take the last of your money," Isaac said.

"This isn't the last. I have other jars in here," Gerald answered.

"Then why live like this if you have all this money?"

"I've always been one who saved my money; plus most of it came from my parents' estate," Gerald explained.

"Your parents are dead?"

"Unfortunately, yes, they are. They died of typhoid last year and left me with a little over six hundred dollars after I had a plot of their land sold off. I still own the house and plan on moving there later on, but until then it sits. I'd move back to Albany, but there's no work there for a cripple like me," Gerald said, referring to his deformed leg. "So take it. I've got more to live off of."

"But the economy? You're only working half the

time you used to," Isaac said.

"Economies go up and down, this recession won't last forever, and as you can see, I live frugally," Gerald said, motioning around the sparsely decorated and furnished apartment.

Knowing he needed the money, Isaac took it and said, "Consider it a loan. I'll pay you back as soon as I can."

"It's not a loan—"

"It is a loan and I'll pay you back," Isaac insisted.

"If that's what you need to tell yourself so you'll take it, then fine. I consider it payment for being a horrible friend the last two years," Gerald said.

Isaac got to his feet and embraced Gerald. "You've always been a dear friend. I understand why you stopped coming, and you paid it all back and then some for having me broken out. I have to say that was easier than I thought it would be."

"It wasn't easy to coordinate," Gerald said.

"I have you to thank; otherwise I would have rotted in there for another sixteen years," Isaac said.

"Can I say anything to convince you to stay away from her?" Gerald asked.

"I'm afraid not," Isaac said. He pocketed the money and headed for the door.

"Will I ever see you again?" Gerald asked.

"I'm not sure. I'd like to think so. If things don't work out, maybe I'll go overseas, to the Orient or the Caribbean."

"I like the sound of that," Gerald said.

"Take care, my friend," Isaac said.

"Take care," Gerald said.

Isaac opened the door, turned and said, "I'll try to stay in contact, so look for a letter sometime in the near future."

"I'll look forward to it," Gerald said with a smile. "And do stop by a tailor shop along the train ride west."

"Why?" Isaac asked.

"I think you're due some new clothes," Gerald said, pointing at Isaac.

Isaac looked down at his old clothes and said, "Good idea."

"Goodbye, my friend," Gerald said.

"Goodbye," Isaac said then stepped out of the apartment, closing the door behind him.

CHAPTER TWO

OCTOBER 26, 1869

CORRIGAN MINING COMPANY OFFICE, BANE, NEVADA

Mortimer jumped to his feet when one of the deputies burst through the door, blood streaming down his face. "Mr. Corrigan, Mr. Corrigan!" the deputy howled.

"Deputy Wallace, what's the matter?" Mortimer asked, his face showing concern.

"Sir, they're dead. They killed them…all," Wallace blared.

"Killed them all? Who? What are you talking about?" Mortimer asked.

"Those bandits, they killed the other deputies. It was horrible," Wallace replied.

"Where?"

"Outside town. We had gathered some credible information that they were planning to hijack a shipment of silver headed to Carson City. We've lost it all, everything, the silver, everything, and all the other deputies are dead."

"They've taken the silver shipment?"

"Yes, sir."

"Didn't Deputy Mace hire some security for the shipment?" Mortimer asked. Mace had been the new deputy in charge until the new sheriff arrived.

"He did, sir. We had the deputies assist in riding out with the shipment, and we had another five men, all heavily armed, but they ambushed us and killed the deputies and all the hired security."

"You're telling me these bandits killed eight well-armed men?" Mortimer asked, shocked by the news.

"That's correct, sir," Wallace replied.

Mortimer could feel the weight of despair and defeat hanging on him. He slowly sat back in the chair and looked at the papers lying there. "The silver, it equaled…" he said but paused before uttering the words of the true value of the loss he'd just experienced.

"Sir, I'm afraid that once some of the hooligans in town get wind that the entire sheriff's office is dead, chaos will grip the streets," Wallace said.

"I need you to go and recruit additional men. We can't let the town be taken over and become lawless again. It's too important; I have someone special coming out to visit soon. We can't let news of the hijacked shipment to also get out. Do you understand?" Mortimer asked.

"How am I supposed to keep that quiet? We both know that it was all Wilkes' men," Wallace said, confirming to Mortimer that Wilkes was the number one suspect behind all the troubles.

"Just do as I ask. As it pertains to Quincy Wilkes, I'll have a word with him concerning this. It's about time I have a formal sit-down with him," Mortimer said.

Wallace stood staring at Mortimer and waited for

further instructions.

"Go, do as I said. Go find some additional men to hire, and make sure we keep the streets of my town safe," Mortimer barked.

Wallace turned and rushed off.

When the door shut, Mortimer lowered his head and placed it in his hands. He was now faced with having to deal with the one man everyone believed was behind the bandits and all the robberies, a man by the name of Quincy Wilkes. Wilkes was the owner of several businesses in town, and his reputation as a hardnosed cutthroat preceded him. The troubles in and outside of town began after his arrival; however, no one could prove it, nor did anyone have evidence. With a major shipment of silver being stolen, this elevated Wilkes' operation and now made him not just a nuisance but a real threat to the future of the town and Mortimer's investment. It was one thing to have food or wares stolen, but silver—that was something that could destroy his enterprise there and prevent him from securing the additional funds from Mr. Wagner, who he had scheduled to come out in eight days' time.

Mortimer looked up at a calendar on the wall and saw the date. He needed his new sheriff more than ever. If Mr. Travis' letter was correct, he'd be in town within four days, and hopefully he'd bring with him the ability to temper this rowdy town and finally stop the bandits and robberies.

He stood up, determined to face Wilkes and deal with it in his own way. Grabbing his hat and coat, he stormed out of the office.

SIXTY-SIX MILES EAST OF ELKO, NEVADA

Isaac stared out the window. He admired the picturesque topography that unfolded before him. Having never traveled outside of the east coast, seeing a great part of the country via the train had been enlightening. What he most marveled over was the desert. From Utah and now into Nevada, the rolling desert hills with the sagebrush was beautiful and mysterious to a man so accustomed to the thick lush green of the eastern states. Soon he'd be ending his train ride once he arrived in Elko. From there he planned on acquiring a horse and riding the additional sixty plus miles to Bane, which was near Tipton Point in the Ruby Mountains.

The door of the railcar opened, bringing in a burst of cold air.

Isaac looked up and saw a tall lean man step in. He was adorned with a large brimmed hat and a thick long trench coat. When the man turned, Isaac spotted a pistol holstered alongside several pouches, which appeared to be holding additional cylinders. He tossed a large leather satchel onto the seat next to a window and plopped down next to it. The man removed his hat, smoothed out his thick tightly cropped black hair, and placed the hat on the satchel.

"Don't stare so much," a man whispered to Isaac in a thick Scottish accent.

Isaac looked back and saw a red-haired man smiling

from ear to ear. "How about minding your own business?"

"I was making sure you don't end up with a bullet in your arse," the man joked.

Isaac shook his head and turned to face the man. "Now why would you say that?"

"On account that I met that bloke a couple of days ago, not a big talker but talked enough. He's a real tough guy, a warrior turned gunman turned lawman."

"Is he now?" Isaac asked, turning his attention back to the man. A fear grew inside him at the mention of him being a lawman.

"Yeah."

"And why would he offer that information up to a complete stranger?" Isaac asked.

"As you can see, I'm not a shy person. I often engage strangers in conversation. It helps break up the monotony of a long trip such as this."

"I suppose it does," Isaac said.

"It's amazing what information people will surrender if you just ask simple questions," the man said.

"And what else did he offer up that's so interesting?" Isaac asked.

"That he's headed to the same place I am," the man answered.

"And where's that?" Isaac asked.

"Bane, Nevada; sort of ironic, isn't it?" the man replied.

"You're headed to Bane?" Isaac asked, shocked to hear the name of the town.

The man cocked his head and, with a twinkle in his deep green eyes, said, "Don't tell me you're headed there too?"

"I am."

"Now that's ironic!" The man laughed.

Isaac offered his hand and said, "I'm Isaac." He instantly regretted using his real first name.

"Connor. Nice to meet you, Isaac," Connor said, taking Isaac's hand and shaking it with vigor. "So what takes you to Bane?"

"I hear there's opportunity," Isaac answered. He wanted to keep any reply as vague as possible.

"It's not working the mines, that's for sure." Connor laughed.

"Why would you say that?" Isaac asked, furrowing his brow.

"On account your hands feel dainty, like you haven't worked a shovel in your life. Not a callus on them," Connor said, holding up his hands to show thick hard calluses. "These are the hands of a hard worker."

Annoyed by Connor's disparaging comment, Isaac turned around and faced the front of the railcar.

"I didn't mean to offend; I was merely making an observation," Connor said.

"I've worked very hard my entire life and spent the last four years..." Isaac said before cutting himself off.

Leaning in, Connor asked, "Last four years doing what?"

Ignoring Connor's question, Isaac asked with a lower tone, "So you traveled all the way from wherever you came from to work in a silver mine?"

"All the way from Scotland, the Highlands up north, to be exact," Connor replied.

Isaac turned back around and asked, "All the way from the Highlands in Scotland to work in a dark silver mine in Nevada?"

"Actually I'm going to Bane to help my older brother, Duncan. He's been there for six months now. He's running a livery. I'm going there to help in the new family business."

"Are Scots known to be horse people?" Isaac asked.

"We are, as well as other things, some I don't dare repeat in respectable company," Connor joked.

The man with the gun shifted in his seat enough to easily look at both Isaac and Connor.

Connor caught his eyes and nodded. "Sheriff."

Isaac looked and said, "Hello, sir."

"You're headed to Bane?" the man asked.

"I am," Isaac replied.

"What do you know about it?" the man asked.

"Not much, it's a mining town owned by a man named Mortimer—"

"Corrigan, yeah, I know who he is. He's the man who hired me to be the new sheriff," the man said.

Isaac leaned across the aisle with his hand extended and said, "My name is Isaac."

The man took his hand and said, "Sheriff Travis. Nice to meet you, Isaac…"

Not wanting to give his real name, Isaac replied, "Isaac Lee."

"Lee like Robert E. Lee?" Travis asked.

"The same, yes, though no relation," Isaac answered, taking his hand back.

"The general is a good man, a great leader," Travis said. "I fought with the Army of Northern Virginia until that sad day in 1865."

"A rebel, huh?" Isaac said.

"Yes, sir. Can I guess you weren't?" Travis asked.

"Union, I was a captain in the Sixty-Seventh New York Volunteer Regiment," Isaac said proudly and unafraid to offer a bit of truth. He couldn't imagine what little information he was sharing could get him caught.

"An officer, impressive. So you're one of those Yanks that comes from an upstanding family?" Travis asked.

When Isaac thought of his family, the word *upstanding* didn't come to mind as a way to describe them. "I just happened to go to college."

"I fought for over three years, entered as a private and left as one. I served with the Fifth Texas Infantry."

"Hood's Brigade! I'm familiar with that. I've heard a lot about you Texans," Isaac exclaimed.

"You know, all of us weren't Texans. Our brigade also had a regiment from Arkansas for a while, some South Carolinians, as well as a Georgia regiment too," Travis said.

"I didn't know that," Isaac said. "I heard many things about the valor of your brigade at Gettysburg."

Travis smiled and looked away.

"The talk about how you Texans fought at Little

Round Top is the stuff of legend," Isaac said with respect.

"We fought hard that day, but came up short," Travis said. "Were you there?"

"Yes, but not at Little Round Top. We were positioned in the Bloody Wheatfield that day," Isaac replied, he too now looking off in deep thought.

"You two have stories to tell, don't you?" Connor blurted out.

Travis smiled and gave Isaac a glance. "It appears we covered much of the same ground."

"It does," Isaac said.

"Did you fight until the end?" Travis asked.

"No, I was wounded outside Spotsylvania, was sent to Washington to recover, then back to New York for further recovery," Isaac replied. "You?"

"I was there when General Lee surrendered at Appomattox. It was a sad day, but I'll admit, I was tired and happy it was over."

"This sounds odd to say, but I haven't met a rebel since the war ended. Of course, I've met sympathizers, many of whom were chicken hawks…" Isaac said.

"What's a chicken hawk?" Connor asked.

"That's a person who talks about going to war but hasn't or won't—all talk and no action," Isaac answered.

Connor nodded.

"So I was saying that I haven't met an actual rebel, one who fought, and I want to say you fought with courage and honor," Isaac said, putting his hand out again to Travis.

Travis looked at Isaac's hand then at him and said, "You haven't traveled much, have you?" Travis then took Isaac's hand and shook.

"This is the furthest I've ever traveled," Isaac said.

Travis pulled his hand back and said, "I'll admit you Yanks were a tough lot, we gave it our all, but you had us beat. I'll admit it took me a year to get over the loss, but I did. When I worked in Pennsylvania as a town marshal, I kept my personal history close to the vest; I didn't want the locals to tar and feather me."

"We Yankees aren't vindictive," Isaac joked.

"Let's not take this conversation there. I've got stories about some carpetbaggers I could share," Travis said.

"Regardless, we're heading to Nevada, and there the memories of war are thousands of miles away," Isaac said.

"Good point," Travis said. "You know, Isaac, I can see us becoming friends."

Connor stuck a flask out and yelped, "That deserves a drink. Who cares for some good Irish whiskey?"

The three all smiled and began to take sips from the flask.

WILKES' OFFICE, BANE, NEVADA

Mortimer was nervous about meeting with Quincy. He'd heard so much about the man, specifically about his reputation. He didn't know what to expect, so he chose to expect the worst.

As he waited in Quincy's office, he took the chance

to look around but found the space lacking décor. The walls were bare of any artwork, and the only furniture in the room was a large oak desk, a swivel chair, and two small armless chairs in front of it.

The door opened and in came a small and round man. He was bald save for a tuft of hair just at the base of his skull. "Mr. Corrigan, so nice to meet you."

Mortimer stood and said, "Mr. Wilkes?"

"That's me. Sorry about the wait. I was busy dealing with some issues," Quincy said, sticking his hand out.

Mortimer took it and shook. He found Quincy's grip to be lacking, it wasn't firm; in fact, it was the opposite, odd for a man who held so much power. "It's quite fine. Thank you for taking the time to meet."

Quincy sat down in the swivel chair. He adjusted his belt to allow for his belly to relax. "I'm sure you're like me, so I'll skip the pleasantries and get to the meat of it all. What can I help you with?"

Mortimer cleared his throat and replied, "I wanted to talk to you about these raids and robberies of stages and supply shipments."

"There's been a lot, I hear. Boy, this town is rowdy. I feel sorry for whoever becomes sheriff. Anyway, how can I help?"

"I'd like to ask you if you know anything about them," Mortimer said. He didn't want to come out and declare Quincy guilty, as he had zero evidence.

Leaning back in his chair, Quincy set his hands on his protruding belly and said, "I've heard about them, hard not to. But I don't know who's doing them or who might be behind these awful things."

"Are you sure?"

"I'm quite sure, Mr. Corrigan, but I'll keep my ear to the ground. I have a lot of people who work for me in this town; I'll ask around for you."

Unconvinced, Mortimer pressed, "Rumors are you're behind them."

Looking shocked, Quincy pointed at himself and blared, "Me!"

"Those are the rumors."

"I can assure you, Mr. Corrigan, I have nothing to do with them or any criminal or unlawful acts in town. I'm a businessman like yourself. I'm here for the opportunity, and thank you for that too."

"You're welcome," Mortimer said. "But as far as these rumors, they're just that and not true, that's what you're telling me?"

"These rumors are false and vile. If I find out who's spreading them, I'll have a word with them," Quincy said.

"Fair enough. I apologize if I've offended you," Mortimer said, getting to his feet.

"Is that it? You wanted to question me about the robberies?" Quincy asked.

"Correct, and you've convincingly defended yourself. If you'll excuse me, I'll let you get back to work."

Jumping to his feet, Quincy said, "If I can help with anything, please don't hesitate to ask."

"Thank you," Mortimer said then headed for the door to leave.

"If I can provide security in the absence of your

deputies, please call upon me," Quincy said.

Mortimer stopped, turned back towards Quincy, and asked, "Who said I needed more deputies?"

Quincy didn't reply right away. He thought for a second then answered, "I heard your deputy put a call out just a bit ago."

"Yes, that's correct," Mortimer replied.

"Is everything alright, Mr. Corrigan?"

"It's fine. We're just beefing up, adding to our ranks. Like you said, this is a rowdy town," Mortimer said and quickly left the office.

As soon as the door closed, a second door near Quincy's desk opened up, and a tall man stepped inside the room. His face was heavily scarred, with one long distinct scar running diagonally from above his right eye down across the bridge of his nose and left cheek, ending just above his upper lip. His name was Marcus Burner and he was Quincy's muscle and right-hand man, who handled everything unsavory.

Quincy looked up and said, "Where's the silver?"

"On its way to Carson City to be sold and have the money deposited into your account at the bank," Marcus answered with a throaty rasp.

"I assume you have it adequately guarded. I don't want what happened to them to happen to us," Quincy said.

"The shipment is safe," Marcus replied.

"Listen, I want you to get some men and take them to the barn where Corrigan has his smelter," Quincy said.

"And?" Marcus asked.

"Burn it down. I don't want him able to smelt his ore here," Quincy said.

"Very well."

"And, Marcus, concerning that new sheriff coming, I don't want him to arrive, do you understand?" Quincy said.

"I'll take care of it personally," Marcus said then sauntered out of the room, exiting out the very door he'd entered from.

Quincy leaned back in his chair. He folded his hands behind his head and smiled.

CHAPTER THREE

OCTOBER 27, 1869

ELKO, NEVADA

After arriving in Elko the evening before, Isaac rented a room at a hotel so he could be properly rested before his two-day ride to Bane.

He wasn't alone in this thinking, as Travis and Connor did the same thing, both staying at the hotel Isaac was in.

All three had enjoyed a dinner together and agreed to ride together to Bane the next morning.

Upon waking early, Isaac went to the local livery and acquired a horse, saddle and saddlebags. Needing a horse as well, Connor joined Isaac at the livery.

Travis, on the other hand, had brought his thoroughbred from Pennsylvania. He was fond of his horse, having had him since just after the war.

Upon riding up to meet Isaac and Connor, Travis saw the horse Isaac was saddling and said, "Nice-looking horse, good color, smart choice."

"You choose by color?" Isaac asked.

"Of course not, but I'm a bit superstitious. I like solid colors, like chestnut, black or gray," Travis said, towering tall in his saddle.

"I'd say she's chestnut," Isaac said, petting the neck of his horse.

Looking around, Travis asked, "Where's Connor?"

"Here," Connor said, walking from the barn with his horse, an older-looking pinto.

"Low on funds, were ya?" Travis laughed.

"All I need to do is get to Bane. There I'll put him in my brother's livery," Connor said.

"If you make the sixty miles to Bane," Travis said, still laughing. "What's the name of the livery?"

"McCarthy Livery and Stables," Connor answered.

Isaac climbed into his saddle and asked, "You reckon it'll take two days?"

"We can do it in two days, but Connor has me worried," Travis said.

"This horse is fine." Connor groaned.

"But yes, two days is doable. We should arrive late tomorrow night or into the early morning hours," Travis said.

"Good," Isaac said.

"You never quite told me what you plan on doing in Bane," Travis said.

Travis was correct, he'd kept his plans vague for fear of stirring up suspicion. "Like I said before, I hear there's opportunity there."

"You're not going to work for the mining company. You seem like a learned man not a laborer," Travis said.

Feeling he needed to offer up something to the man who would eventually be the sheriff of the town, Isaac replied, "Law, I plan on practicing law."

"Law?" Travis chuckled.

"Is that a problem?" Isaac asked.

"It's not a problem. Well, it can be. For a man who wishes to practice law, he needs a town that has laws, and right now Bane is not that sort of town," Travis said.

"He's right, you know," Connor said, mounting his horse. "My brother tells me that men get gunned down almost every night, and there are bandits that torment shipments going in and out of town."

"Hence why I've been hired," Travis said. "They also have a corruption problem, and I aim to tackle that. Maybe you can be the town's magistrate since you have a degree in law."

"I plan on practicing law privately. I have no interest in public service," Isaac said, his stomach tightening at the endless talk about his law background. The last thing he needed was someone looking into him.

"But working for Mr. Corrigan could be more of an opportunity than—"

Cutting Travis off, Isaac barked, "I don't have any interest in public service. Now can we drop it and move out?"

Taken aback by Isaac's forceful response, Travis said with a curious eye on Isaac, "Good idea, let's head out."

Connor also took notice, raising his brow in curiosity at Isaac's reply.

The three rode out of town and headed due south.

CORRIGAN RESIDENCE, BANE, NEVADA

Mortimer was woken by his aide, Edwin, to the news of his smelting facility on fire and a knife fight resulting in a fatality outside the Rusty Nail Saloon.

"Who informed you of this?" Mortimer asked as he tied his robe tightly around him.

"Deputy Wallace, sir," Edwin answered.

"Let's go to my office and finish this conversation," Mortimer said, looking back to the bed to make sure Lucy was still asleep. Seeing she was, he exited the room. Down the hallway he went, his anger building with each step he took. "Did Deputy Wallace hire more people?"

"He did, sir," Edwin answered.

"The fire, what sort of damage are we looking at?" Mortimer asked, stepping into his office.

Edwin came in behind him and closed the double doors. "It appears to be a complete loss."

"Was it arson?" Mortimer asked before answering the question himself. "Of course it was; that's a stupid question."

"Right now we don't know if it is or isn't," Edwin said.

"It is. This is not an accident, you do know that," Mortimer said.

"Sir, I think it's best we don't jump to conclusions," Edwin said calmly.

Frustrated, Mortimer sat in his chair heavily and grunted.

"I do have some good news," Edwin said.

"Good news, please let me hear it," Mortimer said.

"Sheriff Travis arrived last night in Elko; he was leaving this morning. We should expect him to arrive in two days' time."

"He can't arrive soon enough. We need a man of his caliber here now," Mortimer said.

"Sir, can I ask a question concerning the new sheriff?" Edwin asked.

"Sure."

"Rumor is he's a former Confederate and uses a heavy hand when applying the law. Are you worried this approach could backfire?" Edwin asked.

"I don't care if he was a former British soldier who fought in the revolution for the king. He's an experienced lawman and has the reputation for bringing law and order to places that need it," Mortimer replied.

"I was merely asking if you had thought about the political ramifications of such a hire," Edwin said.

"I have thought this through but not politically, and you know why? Because I'm not a mayor, I'm not an elected public servant, this is my town, and I'll do what I want. The entire town, all the land, everything is mine. Let's not forget that. And if people don't like it, they can leave. No one is forcing them to work here. If they leave, I have a line of people wanting to work," Mortimer said.

"Very well," Edwin said.

"Now go. I need to think in private," Mortimer said.

Edwin swiftly exited the room.

Alone, Mortimer swiveled in his chair until he could see outside the window directly behind his desk. There he had a view looking down the main street in town. He liked this personal vantage point and knew the second he looked through it why the house he lived in was built where it was. Having a bird's-eye view on his town, he could always look down on it and watch the people come and go and see it grow when it did. His mind went to the recent troubles. He desperately needed to get everything under control before Everett arrived, and prayed that Sheriff Travis was the right man for the job. While he didn't have the same concerns as Edwin, he did have worries, but his were the opposite. He hoped Travis was as stern as his reputation made him out to be. He felt now that the only thing that could keep the town from falling into the abyss of chaos was a heavy hand.

TWENTY-TWO MILES SOUTH OF ELKO, NEVADA

It had been a very long time since Isaac had ridden a horse any distance, and after doing over twenty miles in the saddle, his butt was as sore as it had ever been.

Seeing Isaac's weary look, Travis said, "Let's stop here for the night, get a good rest, and head out just before dawn."

"Are you sure?" Connor asked, looking west and seeing the sun was still an hour away from setting.

"I'm sure," Travis said.

"I won't disagree," Isaac said, slowing his horse to a trot.

"That flat expanse over there next to the rock outcropping," Travis said, pointing to the left.

The three men made their way to the area and dismounted. They each removed the saddles and gear from their horses and tied them to a stake Travis placed in the ground.

"Connor, do you mind making sure the horses get fed? I've got a feed bag in my left saddlebag. I'll gather some wood for a fire, and Isaac can clear a spot for us to sleep," Travis said.

"I can do that," Connor said, taking a feed bag from Travis' saddlebag.

Isaac didn't say word, his body ached from the long ride, and he was feeling the ride more than he thought he would.

"Are you fine with clearing a spot for us?" Travis asked.

"Sorry, I'm more whooped than I thought I would be. Sure, it's not a problem. I can get the campsite cleared," Isaac said, carrying his saddle over and tossing it on the ground.

Travis looked at Isaac and laughed to himself. There wasn't any doubt to him now that Isaac was more desk than desperado.

***

Isaac was thankful Travis called to stop when he did. His body was aching from the long twenty-mile ride, and a heavy feeling of fatigue permeated him. After eating a hot meal of beans and salted pork, he felt better and knew that once he woke in the morning, he'd be ready to tackle the remaining miles to Bane. Staring at the dancing flames of the fire, his mind raced to Lucy. What was she doing right now? Did she ever think of him? What would she say upon seeing him again?

"You look lost in thought," Travis said as he rubbed a rag along the octagonal barrel of his pistol.

"I'm tired," Isaac replied.

"Did you practice law in New York?" Travis asked.

"I did," Isaac answered, again keeping his answer short of details.

"So if you were gainfully employed, why would a savvy well-spoken lawyer decide to up and leave?" Connor interjected.

"Like I said—"

"Not another thing about opportunity," Connor said.

"It's really as simple as that," Isaac said.

"I've come to know this, people head west for a variety of reasons. Opportunity is one; starting a new life or running away from one is another," Travis said.

"Are you running away from something?" Connor asked.

"If truth be told, I'm coming to see someone I knew long ago, but if it's all the same, I don't want to go into detail," Isaac admitted.

Connor smiled broadly and gave Travis a look and a wink. "What's her name?"

Isaac opened his mouth, but before he muttered the name Lucy, he stopped and said, "Mary, her name is Mary."

"And this Mary is in Bane?" Travis asked.

"It's a long story, but we were supposed to be married, and her father didn't approve. I moved on after that," Isaac replied.

"And now you're coming out here with hopes to win her back?" Travis asked.

"I need to ask her a question, simple as that," Isaac replied.

"You're still in love with her, aren't you?" Connor asked.

"If we can please change the topic, I'd like to do that," Isaac said, regretting he'd even mentioned it.

"Very well," Travis said, taking the cylinder and placing it back in the frame. He reinserted the center pin, locking the cylinder into place, then snapped the loading lever back. He spun the cylinder then lowered the hammer back down.

"That's a Remington, isn't it?" Isaac asked.

"Yes, sir, a New Army," Travis said.

"I prefer Colt," Isaac said.

"Why on earth would you prefer a Colt if you could get a New Army?" Travis asked.

Thinking about it, Isaac replied, "I suppose I like the Colt because it's what I carried during the war."

"I carried a Colt as well, an 1860 Army Colt, but when I got my hands on this Remington, I was convinced this was the best pistol ever made," Travis said as he lovingly admired his pistol.

"Tell me, what's to love about that over the Colt?" Connor asked as he puffed on a pipe.

"It's accurate as hell for one. I like the top strap over the cylinder, which alone makes it more durable to carry, and the ability to quickly reload is unmatched."

"How can you quickly reload a revolver?" Connor

asked, genuinely curious.

"Watch," Travis said. He half-cocked the hammer, lowered the loading lever, pulled the center pin, and popped out the cylinder. He took another cylinder from his gun belt and popped it in, then inserted the center pin, and locked in the loading lever. He cocked it and said, "That fast."

"Impressive. So you carry more than one cylinder?" Connor asked.

"I do. I have four, one in the pistol, and three on my gun belt fully loaded," Travis answered.

Isaac watched Travis with amazement. After having spent years getting his law degree after the war, then more years in prison, he hadn't spent much time shooting. He wasn't entirely unfamiliar with firearms, he was just out of practice. During the war, he'd proven to be quite capable with a rifle and pistol.

"And what do you carry for a long gun?" Connor asked.

"A Winchester," Travis said.

"That's similar to the Henry, isn't it?" Connor asked.

"Better, much better," Travis answered. "The reloading capability of my Yellow Boy far exceeds the Henry."

"A Yellow Boy?" Connor asked.

"That's the nickname given it due to its brass frame," Travis said, pulling his out of the scabbard next to him and tossing it to Connor.

Not expecting the rifle to be thrown, Connor almost dropped it.

"Now be careful. There's one in the chamber, so don't go cocking it," Travis said.

"It's nice," Connor said, admiring the rifle.

"Can I see it?" Isaac asked.

Connor handed it to him butt first.

Like Connor, Isaac admired the rifle. He noted to himself that it looked very similar to the Henry he had seen during the war.

"Are you two not carrying rifles?" Travis asked.

"No, I'm not, didn't think I'd need one," Connor replied.

"Same here," Isaac said then tossed it over the flames of the fire back to Travis' waiting hands.

Travis slid it back in the scabbard and said, "When we get to town, see if you can get your hands on one, and please do yourself a favor, ditch those Colts and get yourself a Remington New Army."

"Say, what does a deputy get paid in a place like Bane?" Connor asked.

"Not sure, but does that question imply you're looking for a job?" Travis asked.

"Maybe, depends on how well it pays," Connor joked.

"No offense, but I prefer to hire veterans or experienced gunmen," Travis said.

"I understand," Connor said.

"Is there a wife in Pennsylvania longingly waiting to receive a telegram from you?" Isaac asked, changing the topic again.

"No wife, or children, at least none that I know of."

Travis laughed.

"I think that's my problem too," Connor said, tipping his flask back.

"And you?" Isaac asked Connor.

"Heavens no, that's not to say I haven't proposed to a few just to get in their knickers," he joked.

A coyote howled in the distance.

The men turned and looked in the direction of the howl.

"What sort of beast was that?" Connor asked.

"A mangy coyote," Travis answered.

"Is that like a wolf?" Connor asked.

"Similar but much smaller, more scavenger than predator, if you ask me," Travis said.

Isaac could feel his eyes getting heavy.

"You're looking bushwhacked; best you shut your eyes. I'll stay up and keep watch for a bit," Travis said.

"Watch?" Connor asked.

"Yeah, while it may seem that we're alone out here, I never take any chances. I didn't come all this way to get murdered in my sleep," Travis said.

"Murdered?" Connor asked. "Who would do that?"

"I'm not sure how life is in Scotland, but out west here, you never know who or what you'll encounter, and the Indians aren't so civil either," Travis said.

Taking Travis up on his offer to watch, Isaac lowered himself down until he was stretched out along his bedroll. He tipped his hat over his eyes and quickly drifted off to sleep.

CORRIGAN RESIDENCE, BANE, NEVADA

Mortimer slipped into the bed and slid close to Lucy, who was pretending to be asleep. He draped an arm over her and nuzzled his face next to her ear. "You don't have to pretend. I know you're awake."

She opened her eyes and said, "I apologize, I'm just tired."

"I'm not here to make love; instead I need your counsel," Mortimer said somberly.

Lucy rolled over and looked at him. "What troubles you?"

"I sometimes wonder if I made a mistake coming here. I dragged you all the way from your life in New York with hopes of carving out a life in this place, but it's been nothing but one obstacle after another. I've worked so hard to get this profitable, only to have my latest silver shipment stolen."

"Wait, your silver shipment was stolen?" she asked, sincerely shocked and concerned by the news.

"Yes, and now someone burned down our smelting facility. No one was killed, but they destroyed everything. It will cost me a lot to replace what was lost. Now I'll have to ship the ore to Carson City instead of the extracted silver."

Taking his hand, she said, "If you're worried about how my father will look at this, I can say that he's an understanding man. He's been through ups and downs, especially during the war years. I think he'll see the recent issues as something that can be fixed and not hold back his desire to invest in the mining operations."

"Are you sure?"

"I'm not one hundred percent sure, but my father is a smart businessman who's able to sniff out a good deal versus a bad one, and this is not a bad one," she said.

"I'm just praying that this new sheriff will be just what we need to get this town back in order," Mortimer said.

"You said he comes with a reputation for tackling such things, so we should be fine. I suggest that you give him great leeway to run his office and his deputies. Men like him don't like to be managed, if you know what I mean?"

"I know what you mean, and I'll fight my inclination to control him," Mortimer said.

"You've been working so hard since we arrived, and I do appreciate everything you do, but if you ever want to leave, I'll support your decision," Lucy said.

"Listen, I know our marriage wasn't what you really wanted. I know that you loved another before me and that it would take time for me to win you over. I just pray that you at least give me a chance, an honest chance, to do just that. I so want to have children, and we can't if you withhold your love from me. It's been so long since we—"

She placed her index finger on his lips so he'd stop talking. "I will honor my wifely duties when I feel well, but you know I've been ill. When I feel better, I'll do what's needed."

"Lucy, we've been married three years now, and still

we don't have a child. You're not getting any younger, and the longer you wait, the more problematic it can be."

"Don't listen to silly doctors," she said.

"But they're the ones who know."

"I know my body better than any doctor. When the time is right and I'm well, we will try to have a child," she said.

"Is the medicine helping with your anxiety and migraines?" he asked.

"It is, but these things take time," she lied.

"It's been almost nine months since we were together," he complained.

Taking his hand and squeezing it gently, she said, "I promise you, when I feel well, I will be the wife you deserve." She hated even having to say it. She didn't love him, but she also didn't hate him. She knew that eventually she'd have to give him the child he so wanted. The one person she did hate was her father for forcing her to marry a man she didn't care for. After Isaac, she'd fallen into a depression, which Everett thought it best to remedy with a wedding against her wishes. Now three years later, her depression was worse with no hope of subsiding.

"You say that to me every time we talk about this. I'm your husband and deserve more," he complained.

"You have my permission to seek that which I'm denying you somewhere else. I just ask that you do so with discretion," she said.

"I don't want anyone else, I want you," he pleaded.

"But, Mortimer, I don't feel well," she again lied.

"Can you just let me…?"

She pulled her hand back and said, "Do you want to make love to me, or do you just seek to use my body?"

"I…"

"I know what you were asking, and if you loved me, you'd leave me be until I feel better," she said, rolling back over and showing him her back.

"That's not what I meant," he said.

"Leave me be. I'm tired and I'm now getting a headache," she groaned.

Frustrated with every aspect of his life, he hastily got out of bed, threw on his robe, and made his way to his office. There he opened a decanter of brandy and poured. Unlike himself, he tossed the full glass back and poured himself another. Like before, he drank it with one gulp. He snatched the decanter in his left hand and walked to his desk. Plopping down, he filled his glass once more, but this time he didn't drink it right away. He leaned back in the chair and stared out the window. Down on the dimly lit street beyond, he could make out people walking in and out of the saloons and gambling houses. He wondered if they were as unhappy as he was, or were poverty and ignorance truly blissful? What he had always wanted in his life was a joyful and content home life filled with happiness, a doting wife, and playful children; instead what he had was a house where he felt like an intruder and a wife who desired her medicine and solitude more than him. Disgusted at the thought, he drank the third glass, but instead of refilling it, he tossed it across the room. The glass smashed upon hitting the wall.

He had nothing in his life that brought him joy. Just when he began to think the mining operations would begin to turn a profit, he was literally robbed. He couldn't figure out where he'd gone wrong, but something was amiss. He'd gone from being a happy and successful bachelor to an unhappily married man whose business venture was teetering on the edge.

He tightly pressed his eyes closed and thought of how he could turn it around. Where was that moment, that person, that event that would signal a shift in the momentum? He needed it more than ever and soon, or he felt he'd come apart at the seams.

CHAPTER FOUR

OCTOBER 28, 1869

TWENTY-TWO MILES SOUTH OF ELKO, NEVADA

As Isaac packed up his horse, Connor approached him and said, "I'm really not prying, but you should try hiding those wrists better."

Isaac looked down at his wrists and the thick scars on them. He hadn't thought much of rolling up his sleeves, but with Connor saying something, he quickly rolled them down.

"I'm sure the sheriff here didn't see, and don't you worry, your secret is safe with me," Connor said, winking.

"And what secret do you think that is?" Isaac asked.

Pulling up one of his sleeves and showing some scars, Connor answered, "It appears we've both spent time behind iron bars."

"I don't know what you're talking about. I got those from the war," Isaac said, turning away from Connor so he could get back to preparing his horse for the day's ride.

"You were a prisoner of war?" Connor asked.

"How about you mind your own business?" Isaac said.

"Listen, I'm just trying to help you out here. If the sheriff sees those marks, he's liable to get curious, and I can assume you're out for time served or parole, but if you escaped, then having the sheriff sniffing around won't be in your best interest."

Isaac turned around and said, "I didn't escape. I'm not what you think I am."

"So it's parole or time served, eh?" Connor asked, picking up on Isaac's comment about not escaping.

"Leave me alone," Isaac snapped.

"Let me just give you some advice. Most people don't care if you served your time; to them you're still a criminal and they'll always look at you that way. If you did come out here to start new, first thing you should do is keep your past to yourself, hide those wrists, and if you're good at lying, become a totally different person, if you know what I mean."

Isaac stared at Connor, anger welling up inside him.

Connor winked again and sauntered off.

The anger Isaac was feeling wasn't because Connor was out of line; it was the opposite, he was correct. He knew no one would ever look at him with trust or offer real friendship if they knew he'd been imprisoned for years, no matter what he said or how passionately he declared his innocence. It was a natural human trait to judge and look down on others; heck, he'd been guilty of that himself before. It definitely felt different now that he was the one who could be held in judgment. He looked over his shoulder at Travis and frowned. He had already given up too much information, and Bane was no doubt a small town. Soon word would spread that a man named Isaac, an attorney from New York and veteran of the war, was there looking for his long-lost love. Aggravated that he'd allowed himself to reveal so much of his life, he gritted his teeth and began to ponder if he should even be making this ride. What would happen if he did arrive in town and his true identity was confirmed? He'd be arrested immediately and possibly hanged, those were things he heard happened in the west. Law and order was practiced differently out here.

Travis appeared behind him. "I see your thoughts plague you again."

Jolted back to the present, Isaac turned around and said in a stutter, "I-I, um, yes, I'm just thinking about the long ride."

Patting him on the shoulder, Travis said, "It's the woman, isn't it?"

Shaking his head, Isaac answered, "No, it's not."

"I once knew a girl named Mary back in Austin. A real sweet thing, knew her before the war. At the time I thought we could possibly get married, but then Lincoln called up those volunteers, and before I knew it, Texas had seceded and I was off to war."

"Did she marry someone else?" Isaac asked.

"Oh no, nothing like that. Poor Mary died of typhus."

Shocked, Isaac said, "I'm sorry to hear that."

"I was sorry to receive that news too. The sorrow of it all is I didn't know she had died until ten months after her death. The damn Confederacy's mail service was the worst."

"Ours was pretty bad too."

Drifting off in thought, Travis could see Mary in his mind's eye. Shaking off the painful memories, he said, "You ready to head out?"

"I am," Isaac said.

"Good man," Travis said. He turned but stopped and looked back. "I look forward to getting to know you more once we get to Bane. It will be nice to swap some war stories. I'm sure we faced off in more places than Gettysburg."

"I'm sure we did too," Isaac said with a fake smile stretched across his face. He hated that Travis wished to get to know him more. He wanted nothing but the opposite, and that was to be as far away from him as possible.

WILKES' OFFICE, BANE, NEVADA

Quincy paced his office, reciting a speech he was about to deliver to a group of investors he was trying to convince to give him the balance of the money he needed to acquire an adjacent plot of land next to Bane. He'd sent out teams of men recently to scout several plots, and this one appeared to have the ore he was looking for. If he could get it, it would set him up as a rival to Mortimer and the town of Bane. He wanted nothing more than to own an operation like that; being the proprietor of various small businesses wasn't enough for him.

A tap on the door pulled him away from his thoughts. "Yes."

Marcus stepped into the room and closed the door.

Stopping his back and forth, Quincy asked, "What do you want? I'm busy here."

"I thought you should know that the shipment of silver we hijacked was stolen early this morning," he said stoically.

"Excuse me?"

"We lost the silver," Marcus said.

"How is that possible? You said we had adequate security," Quincy said.

"We did, more than enough…"

"It clearly wasn't enough, damn it," Quincy howled. "I needed that silver to help with my position on the parcel of land and the mining company. Damn it all to hell!"

"I'm sending out a few men to scout for where it went and who did it," Marcus said.

Quincy rushed over to Marcus and jabbed his index finger into his hard muscular chest. "Find that silver!"

Marcus looked down at Quincy and at his finger.

Sensing that Marcus didn't like being touched, Quincy stopped and took a few steps back. "Are you going to be able to find my silver, or do I need to get someone else to do it?"

"I'll find it," Marcus said.

"When you catch who took it, I want their head, I mean that literally," Quincy barked.

"Yes, sir."

"Now go," Quincy grunted.

"I also got word from a contact in Elko; the new sheriff is en route. I'll take care of him before he arrives,"

Marcus said.

"Good, and don't mess that up, you understand me?" Quincy growled.

Marcus simply nodded then turned and exited the office.

When the door closed, Quincy walked to his desk and shoved the items that sat on it onto the floor. "Damn it!"

CORRIGAN MINING COMPANY OFFICE, BANE, NEVADA

Edwin stopped just before knocking on Mortimer's office door. He had more bad news to deliver and pondered if telling him was prudent.

The door opened abruptly, startling Edwin.

"What are you doing hovering at my door?" Mortimer asked, his brow furrowed.

"I was just about to knock, sir," Edwin said, clearing his throat.

"Walk with me. I'm headed to the bank to sign some documents," Mortimer said and pushed past Edwin and down the hall.

Edwin turned and followed Mortimer outside.

Rushing across the bustling street, Mortimer asked, "What did you need to see me about?"

"Sir, I received word that Quincy Wilkes has four wealthy businessmen arriving on November 1. They're coming in on the stage from Carson City," Edwin replied.

"He does, does he?" Mortimer asked, his pace

increasing to get past a horse coming his way.

"Yes, sir, and the word is these men are coming to invest in a plot of land adjacent to Bane to the south. It's approximately two thousand acres."

Arriving at the bank door, Mortimer stopped and asked, "And what does Mr. Wilkes want with this land?"

"My source has told me that he's found deposits of ore," Edwin answered.

"Where is this land, and who's selling it?" Mortimer asked.

"Sir, I'll try to get that to you later," Edwin replied.

"Good, because I want to see it as soon as you can," Mortimer said. "Is there anything else?"

"Yes, one more thing, where did you want me to have the new sheriff live?" Edwin asked.

"Where the old sheriff lived," Mortimer said.

"Sir, you let the old sheriff's family stay there after his death. Don't you remember?"

Mortimer rubbed his chin, his mind spinning over past conversations. "I think I vaguely recall."

"I can set him up in the hotel until I find a house," Edwin said.

"No, don't do that. Give him the downstairs suite in my house. I want to keep him close for a while, get to know him. That'll give you time to find adequate housing for him," Mortimer said.

"Very well, sir," Edwin said.

"If that's it, I need to go see the bank manager," Mortimer said.

"That's it, sir," Edwin said.

"Oh, I almost forgot. Who is this source?"

"Excuse me, sir?"

"You referenced a source. Who is it, and how come they know about Mr. Wilkes' business dealings but can't confirm if he's the one behind the robberies and other mayhem in town?" Mortimer asked.

"I don't think it's prudent to give away his identity," Edwin said.

"Edwin, you work for me, and that means you divulge all you know. I don't have time now, but I expect to know who this source is tomorrow. Do you understand? I also want you to dig further into this parcel of land Wilkes is trying to acquire."

"Yes, sir," Edwin said.

"Good, now go back to the house and make sure that Phyllis has the room ready for our guest and inform Lucy we'll be having the new sheriff staying with us for the next few days," Mortimer ordered.

"Yes, sir, I'll get right on it," Edwin said, nodding before rushing off.

Mortimer liked the idea of having Travis at his house for a few days. This would give him the ability to have in-depth conversations with the man and get to know him better.

TEN MILES NORTHWEST OF BANE, NEVADA

Travis looked back over his shoulder and could see Isaac waning, as was Connor. They were so close, but he knew his traveling partners were hurting. He slowed his horse to a stop and called out, "Shall we stop for a few hours?"

"How much farther?" Isaac asked.

"I'm guessing about eight to ten miles since we're close to entering the pass up the mountains," Travis replied.

"I could use a break," Connor said, catching up to Isaac.

"But we're close, let's see this through," Isaac said to him.

"Fine, let's take a break here for a couple of hours then finish. We should make it to Bane by midnight," Travis said, dismounting.

Isaac and Connor rode up.

"Are you sure? I would rather just suffer through these last miles and get there earlier," Isaac said.

Slowly getting off his horse, Connor moaned. "Sorry, but my arse needs a break from this saddle."

Isaac's butt and back hurt as well, but he was serious when he said he just wanted to finish the ride.

Travis secured his horse to a stake and removed its saddle along with his other gear.

Connor followed his lead.

Relenting to the fact he was going to be taking a break, Isaac got off his horse and tied it up. He gave his horse some water and hitched up the feed bag.

Plopping to the ground hard, Connor grunted. "Oh, my aching arse."

"We don't need a fire. Let's relax, stretch our backs and set out at sunset," Travis said, taking a seat and leaning against his saddle.

Isaac joined the two, setting his kit next to Connor. The two sparked up a casual conversation, which went on for a few minutes. When they noticed Travis was unusually quiet, they looked over and saw he was sleeping.

"Looks like he might have needed the rest more than us." Connor chuckled.

"If you want to catch some sleep, go ahead. I'll stay awake," Isaac offered.

"Tell me, what did you do?" Connor whispered.

"Do? What are you referring to?" Isaac asked.

"To go to prison?" Connor asked, keeping his voice just above a whisper.

Isaac's face turned stern. He shot a look over at Travis then back at Connor. "Keep your voice down."

"It is down; that's why I'm whispering," Connor said.

"I'm not talking about this now or ever with you," Isaac growled under his breath.

"I accidentally killed a man in a pub. Hit him over the head with a pint glass, but it wasn't the hit that killed him. The poor bastard fell backwards and impaled his temple on a nail that was jutting out of the corner of the bar," Connor said. "He said something about my mother, and I don't take kindly to anyone's mother being mentioned in a derogatory fashion, especially my own," Connor said, taking his flask from his pocket. He unscrewed the top and handed it first to Isaac, who waved it away, then took a swig. After wiping his mouth, he continued, "I was jailed for three years. Upon my release, I set sail for America."

"I suppose you're lucky to be alive," Isaac said, referring to the death penalty for killing.

"I was, the bastard happened to be the town agitator. Fortunately for me, no one liked him, specifically the judge whose daughter the man had bedded some six months before that." Connor laughed.

"They let the judge hear the case?" Isaac asked.

"Of course, why wouldn't they?"

"On account that he was clearly prejudiced," Isaac replied.

"You're clearly not aware of how small the village I came from is. He was the only judge around for a hundred miles. Anyway, the rotten bastard deserved what he got. I was heralded a hero as such, but regardless of my newfound status in the village, I didn't want to go back to that life. Upon hearing my family—including my mother, whose honor I had defended that day—went to America, I had to join them."

"They abandoned you?"

"Oh, I wouldn't call it abandonment, no. Their coming to America allowed me to leave that vile place with hopes and dreams of a better life," Connor said, taking a swig. "How did your family take it when you went away?"

Scowling at Connor, Isaac shot a look at Travis again, this time noticing he was now snoring slightly.

"You were serious, weren't ya?" Connor asked.

"I was, I'm not saying anything about anything," Isaac said.

"Did you kill someone?" Connor taunted.

"No, I didn't kill anyone," Isaac fired back.

"Robbery? Wait, you're a smart man, schooled no doubt at a good institution, I'd say it must have been some sort of crime involving money. Did you get creative with accounting?"

Isaac jumped to his feet and walked off. He didn't want to listen to Connor taunt him.

"Oh, c'mon. Keep your head, would ya!" Connor yelped.

Isaac waved his hand, dismissing Connor. He walked to a large boulder and climbed on top of it. From there he had a nice vantage point of the long sloping valley to the north and south of him. He could now see that for the past few hours they had been riding up a long and gentle incline. He spun his head around and looked at the foothills and mountains beyond. Soon they'd be headed up a long and winding trail to the town of Bane, which sat at an elevation of forty-three hundred feet. He didn't know what to expect upon his arrival in town, but he was anxious to get there, not only to see Lucy but to get away from both Travis and Connor.

FIVE MILES NORTHWEST OF BANE, NEVADA

"It's a good thing there isn't a full moon." Connor chuckled.

"Why's that?" Isaac replied.

"On account that to the right, it's a thousand-foot drop," Connor answered.

Hearing that, Isaac pulled the reins of his horse and navigated it to the left side of the trail. He looked to his right and could make out a drop-off under the light of the half-moon but couldn't see the bottom.

"It's not that far down," Travis said. "I reckon it's maybe a few hundred feet."

"That doesn't make me feel better. You can die from a hundred-foot fall just the same as a thousand-foot fall," Isaac said.

"Listen, just take it slow and trust your horse," Travis said.

A loud clang sounded as a couple of items fell from Isaac's horse.

"What was that?" Travis asked, slowing his horse to a stop.

Isaac looked back but couldn't see. "I think something fell off my horse. It might have been my canteen and the feed bag. I hastily tied them to the saddlebags just before leaving."

"Well, go get them," Travis said.

"You go ahead. I'll catch up," Isaac said, dismounting.

"No, we'll wait," Travis said.

"If I get off the horse, I'm not sure I can get back on again," Connor said, complaining about his sore muscles.

"No, please go ahead. I've got to take care of some other business too," Isaac said, walking back to find his canteen on the ground.

"He means he has to have a bowel movement." Connor laughed.

"We'll go ahead. Just holler when you're coming," Travis said, turning his horse and trotting up the trail.

"I'm a jealous man. I haven't had a movement since Elko," Connor joked before trotting off.

The two rounded a corner and disappeared out of view.

Isaac kicked the dirt and small rocks around him, looking for the feed bag. "Where are you?" He spotted something dark near the edge of the trail. He walked over, stopping suddenly when he noticed the feed bag was literally at the edge of the drop-off. He cautiously bent down and picked it up. Stepping away from the edge, he looked around for anything else.

A volley of gunfire erupted up the trail ahead of him. Frozen from the shock, he stared down the dimly lit trail.

Another volley of gunfire followed.

This time he acted. He ran to his horse, climbed on, and ripped his Colt from his holster. He cocked it then kicked the horse with his spurs, driving it forward.

The horse lunged ahead and sprinted towards the gun battle that was now raging, as he could hear Travis and Connor returning fire.

Connor howled in what sounded like pain then went silent followed by an eerie silence.

Isaac rounded the corner but couldn't see anything. He nudged the horse more forcefully. "Go!"

The horse responded by opening up its stride.

The turn ahead was shaped like an S. When Isaac came out of it, he saw a dark mass lying in the trail with some movement in front of it. He called out, "Travis, is that you?"

The dark mass stopped.

A crack of a weapon sounded.

Isaac could hear the round ball whiz by him. He raised his Colt, took aim and squeezed. The pistol fired, launching a .44-caliber round ball towards the mass. He heard the round hit whoever it was. They dropped to the ground.

Another crack of a weapon came from above him.

Like before, the round traveled just past him. He looked and saw movement. He cocked the pistol, aimed and fired. Again his aim was true, and the round ball struck the man. Seeing two more above him, he cocked and fired.

"Let's get, c'mon," a man cried out from the rock outcropping above the trail.

Isaac looked, but it was very difficult to see. He could hear what sounded like two men running above him on the rocks but couldn't see them. He sat in the saddle, ready to engage, but didn't as the footfalls grew more distant then disappeared.

Frantic, Isaac swiveled his head around, looking for anything or anyone that could be a threat but found nothing but the cold dark night. He uncocked his Colt before dismounting. On the ground he went to the first person he saw, not knowing who it was until he was a foot away. "Connor?" he called out. He knelt down and felt Connor's neck to see if there was a pulse. Finding one, he said, "How bad are you hurt?"

"I fell," Connor replied, his voice sounding groggy.

"Are you shot?" Isaac asked, checking for any wounds.

"I don't think so," Connor answered, staring up into the starlit sky. "They shot my horse out from underneath me. I toppled off it and struck my head on a rock."

Isaac felt the back of his head. "You're bleeding."

"I must have cut my head open," Connor said. "That's odd."

"What's odd about it?" Isaac asked.

"On account I've been told I have a hard head all my life," Connor said, managing to find a joke even after the intense gunfight.

Isaac looked around and spotted who he thought was Travis. "Let me go check on Travis." He jumped up and rushed over to find Travis lying facedown. Grabbing his shoulder, he turned him onto his back. Like he had with Connor, he check for a pulse but couldn't feel one. Travis' face appeared dark, unrecognizable. He looked closer and recoiled when he saw that he had a hole where his nose used to be. "He's dead."

"Huh?" Connor said, still lying on his back.

"Travis is dead, shot in the face," Isaac said, sighing.

"Who do you suppose they were?"

"I'm not sure, but we need to get moving."

"I was thinking the same thing," Connor said, sitting up and grunting in pain as he reached over his shoulder and touched the back of his head.

Isaac got his horse and walked it over to Travis. "Help me get him on the back of the horse."

"Why?" Connor asked.

"'Cause we're not going to leave him lying on this trail. We're going to take him to town and give him a decent Christian burial," Isaac declared.

Connor shuffled over and took Travis' legs.

Isaac grabbed Travis underneath his armpits and said, "Up."

The two men lifted him up and set him on the back of Isaac's horse.

"Where's his horse?" Connor asked, looking around.

"There, I think," Isaac said, pointing to a dark mass farther down the trail.

Connor walked to it and said, "Now settle down." He rubbed the horse's neck and mumbled something unintelligible in its ear.

With Travis secured to his horse, Isaac looked around on the ground for weapons. He picked one up and saw it was Travis' Remington. He shoved it in his waistband and continued looking. He found a Colt, which must have been Connor's, and took the weapon off the man he'd killed on the trail.

"Let's get moving," Connor called out.

Isaac shoved the other pistols into a saddlebag, mounted his horse and said, "Lead the way."

"I was hoping you'd take charge," Connor replied.

CHAPTER FIVE

OCTOBER 29, 1869

TRIPLE B HOTEL, BANE, NEVADA

Marcus was awoken by the sound of banging on his door. He shoved the sleeping prostitute off him and swung his legs out of the bed. Reaching over, he turned up the kerosene lantern. Light filled the small bedroom.

More banging at the door.

"Who is it?" he called out.

"It's Phillip," a man replied, his voice sounding frenzied.

The prostitute touched Marcus' back and purred, "Where are you going?"

Ignoring her, he stood up, slipped on his long underwear, and grabbed his Colt Dragoon from the nightstand. He sauntered to the door and unlocked it. Swinging it open, he said, "What is it?"

"The sheriff, we gunned him down along with another man," Phillip said.

"Why are you telling me this? Where's Cornelius?" Marcus asked, referring to the man he had put in charge of the ambush.

Removing his sweat-stained hat, Phillip said, "Cornelius didn't make it. He was killed."

"Did you dispose of his body?" Marcus asked.

Looking at the floor, Phillip nervously answered,

"No, but…"

"Why not? We can't have the bodies of any man that can be connected to me or Mr. Wilkes lying out on the road."

"Well, you see, we couldn't on account that other riders came up and chased us off," Phillip lied, hoping that his exaggerated story would be enough to convince Marcus of why they had failed to fulfill their obligation.

"Who's the handsome friend?" the prostitute cooed from the bed.

Hearing the woman, Phillip stuck his head in the room and raised his brow in excitement. "Sorry to disturb you, ma'am."

Angry, Marcus shoved him across the hallway and stepped out of the room, closing the door behind him. "Are you sure you killed the new sheriff?"

"Yes, we're sure?"

"How? Did you get a confirmation?" Marcus asked.

"Um, you see, Cornelius went down after we shot them to confirm, but those riders appeared and killed Cornelius as well as John W."

"John's dead too?"

"Yes," Phillip answered, swallowing hard.

Unable to control his anger, Marcus cocked his Dragoon and shoved it under Phillip's jaw. "I should blow your brains out."

"Don't do that, please," Phillip begged.

"I sent you all out there to do a simple job. Now turn around and go back out there. Take more men with you and confirm you killed the sheriff."

"Yes, sir," Phillip said and hurried off.

Marcus cursed under his breath. He went back into his room and slammed the door.

"Since you're awake, why don't you come over here," the prostitute said.

Marcus walked over to the bedside and set his pistol down. He took the woman forcefully by the jaw and squeezed. "Don't ever talk to any of my men, do you understand?"

Wide-eyed with fear, she cried out, "Yes."

He let go of her by shoving her into the pillows. He took his trousers, which dangled from the footboard, and put them on.

"Are you leaving?" she asked.

"I am and so are you. Get your clothes on," he barked.

She hopped out of bed, grabbed what few clothes she had, and rushed out of the room.

Marcus tried to think how he'd explain to Quincy if the sheriff hadn't been killed. He personally guaranteed it would be done, and that meant he should have been there to ensure it happened. Now he'd have to tell him that he'd delegated the responsibility, which he knew would be met with spiteful anger.

For him there was nothing worse than being on the receiving end when Quincy went on a tirade.

When he finished getting dressed, he holstered his pistol, grabbed his hat, and exited the room. Before he'd subject himself to ridicule from a man the likes of Quincy, he'd at least head out with Phillip and the other men to confirm the sheriff's death and, if need be, correct the error.

TWO MILES NORTHWEST OF BANE, NEVADA

"How are we going to explain this?" Connor asked.

"Explain what? We were ambushed by bandits, it's simple," Isaac replied.

"Two former convicts bringing in the body of the new sheriff, that doesn't sound good," Connor said.

"No one knows who we are or where we've come from," Isaac said, though he began to grow concerned.

"Think about it, Isaac; don't be daft. They might look at us. In the absence of suspects and no witnesses, they might choose to hang us for his killing," Connor said sincerely.

Isaac pulled back on the reins until his horse stopped. He looked at Connor and asked, "Do you really think they'd arrest us?"

"Tell me, how did you end up in prison? And don't give me a song and dance," Connor asked.

Isaac sighed and said, "I told you before, I'm not discussing this."

"You seem to me like a man who was falsely imprisoned, don't ask me how I know, but you come across as very angry about your incarceration."

"And how would you even pretend to know such a thing?"

"On account that you're a righteous arse."

"Maybe I'm not proud of that period of my life,"

Isaac said.

"Think about it and stop pretending with me. If we ride into town with the new sheriff slung over a horse, we'll be the first two they suspect."

"What sort of suspects take the man they murdered to town to report it?" Isaac asked, challenging Connor's theory.

Tapping his temple, Connor replied, "Two former convicts would, hoping that their story would be believed."

"Are you drunk?" Isaac asked.

"No, but I don't trust a single person, including you," Connor said.

"Then what are you proposing we do?" Isaac asked.

"We dump his body down that ravine, no body, no questions. By the time anyone finds it, if they ever do, we'll be long cemented into the fabric of the town."

Isaac grunted his displeasure with Connor but began to think about the possibilities of being once more wrongfully accused of a crime he hadn't committed. And if they were suspects, someone could find out he was an escaped convict. This one would result in his hanging from a rope instead of serving time.

"You're thinking I'm right, aren't you?" Connor asked.

"I'm thinking you're crazy," Isaac said.

"But right," Connor shot back.

"You might be right, but dumping his body isn't right. If we go into town without him, we bury him and say a few words," Isaac said.

"Bury him? He's dead. He doesn't care if he's buried or food for critters. Why waste the time? And I'm sore as hell," Connor complained.

"We either bury him or take him into town," Isaac declared.

Connor grumbled then said, "You Yankees, so damn righteous."

***

Finding a spot high above the trail, Connor and Isaac dug a shallow grave with their bare hands. They laid Travis' body in it and paused.

Isaac looked at him and said, "I didn't get to know you, but you were a good man."

Removing his hat, Connor said, "May the good Lord bless you and keep you. And when you find the pearly gates, tell Saint Peter I'll be seeing him in forty or so years."

Isaac shook his head, dismayed by Connor's prayer.

The sun crested the horizon. Its rays began to warm their faces.

Looking at Travis, Isaac spotted his badge. A thought came to him. He bent down and removed it.

"Keepsake?" Connor asked.

Isaac reached into his jacket pocket, found his wallet, and took it out.

"How about you split what he has with me?" Connor said.

"I don't want his money, I want his papers," Isaac

said.

Connor got on his knees and began to pat Travis' pockets.

"What are you doing?" Isaac asked.

"Seeing if he has anything else of value," Connor said.

"So you're going to rob him?"

"What do you call what you're doing?" Connor shot back.

"I was going to...I don't know; I was thinking I could send this back to his family in Texas maybe," Isaac said.

Shaking his head vigorously, Connor laughed. "And to think, I was the one who hit my head."

"He didn't say he didn't have family," Isaac countered.

"And who will be sending this letter?" Connor asked.

"It will be anonymous," Isaac said.

"With a postmark from Bane, it could get people looking; maybe even bring some of those Pinkertons sniffing about," Connor said. "Jackpot!" Connor exclaimed when he found a pocket watch.

"Are all Scotsman like you?" Isaac asked.

"Do you mean handsome and dashing?" Connor joked.

Turning around, Isaac went to gather some stones to cover the body.

"You know, if I were you, I wouldn't send his papers and badge to his family, if they even exist," Connor said.

Hauling a large stone back, Isaac asked, "I suppose

you'd try to sell it?"

"What's the one thing we ex-convicts want more than anything else?" Connor asked.

"I know I want you to shut up and help me," Isaac said, setting the stone down on Travis' body.

"To be someone new," Connor said.

Isaac stopped and looked at Connor. "Are you saying I should take his identity?"

"You've come all this way with hopes to sweep this lass off her feet. This woman isn't going to fall into your arms. Who are you fooling? She's in Bane because years ago you were convicted of a crime, and let me say this before you interrupt me, it doesn't matter if you were wrongfully jailed, the reality is you were. She'll never be yours again, but if you ever…ever want the chance at love again and to find a woman—a respectful woman—you can't be Isaac the ex-convict. You should be Sheriff Ethan Travis, the lawman. Because that's a man people look up to, that's a man a woman can fall in love with."

CORRIGAN RESIDENCE, BANE, NEVADA

Lucy opened her eyes and stared at the bottle of laudanum. Deep down she reviled the person she'd become. Never would she have ever imagined herself becoming addicted to such a substance. She'd heard about people falling victim to it, but would never have seen herself as one of those weak-willed individuals. Yet here she was, longingly ogling the dark brown bottle, its contents providing her the ability to even manage the trifling and meaningless life she was trudging through daily.

Like every morning, she rose slowly, swung her legs out of the bed, and took the bottle. She administered herself her dose then sat until she could feel it providing her relief.

From the bed she walked to her vanity and sat down. As she brushed her hair, she contemplated what she'd do today. Should she take a walk in town or maybe read? Mortimer had purchased her a set of books, which she hadn't opened yet; maybe today was a good day to start a new book.

A tap on the door tore her away from her trivial thoughts. "Yes."

"Ma'am, it's Phyllis. May I have a word with you?"

"Come in," Lucy said.

The door opened and in came Phyllis. She was an older woman, late fifties, with thick silver hair pulled back into a tight bun. "Ma'am, I was hoping to get some direction from you concerning supper tonight."

"Whatever you want to make," Lucy said, running the stiff bristles of the brush through her thick brown hair.

"Since we're having a special guest, I thought I should ask you, ma'am," Phyllis said.

Stunned to hear about a special guest, Lucy turned towards Phyllis and asked, "Is it my father?"

"No, ma'am, it's not your father; my understanding is he's arriving on November 3. I'm referring to the new sheriff. I received word that he would be staying in the downstairs room for a few days, maybe more."

"The new sheriff, hmm, why didn't Mortimer tell me?" Lucy asked herself out loud.

"What do you recommend I make?"

"How about making a beef roast with fingerling potatoes," Lucy said, finding it exciting that a guest would be staying at the house. Having someone new would break up the monotony.

"Very well, ma'am, I'll head to the butcher and get the meat. Will you be needing me the next couple of hours?"

"No, you may go and, Phyllis, make sure we have wine and sherry," Lucy said.

"Yes, ma'am," Phyllis said, closing the door as she left.

Lucy pivoted back until she could see herself fully in the mirror of her vanity. "A guest. I wonder what the sheriff is like?"

BANE, NEVADA

Isaac and Connor slowed their horses to a trot when they entered the main street of town.

Isaac scanned the face of each woman that passed by him, hoping to see Lucy. However, if he happened to see her, he wasn't sure if he'd cry out for her. What would she say to him? Would she want to see him? The entire ride to town since burying Travis, he'd pondered what Connor had told him to do. He never acknowledged that he'd do what was suggested, but it did sound tempting.

Just being in Bane and meeting with Lucy was a huge gamble for him. He didn't know what she was like or if she even still liked him. What if she hated him for being imprisoned? What if in a fit of anger she reported him? The risk was there, but he was willing to take it so he could see her one more time.

Seeing the two men entering town, Edwin jumped up from the barber's chair, shaving cream still lathered on his face, and ran out the door. "Sheriff Travis, is that you?"

Hearing the name, Isaac looked at Connor and asked, "What should we do?"

"Act casual, not get jumpy. Have you decided what you're going to do?" Connor asked.

"I don't know. Should we ride over to the man?" Isaac asked.

"Sheriff Travis, is that you?" Edwin asked again, stepping down from the wooden walkway and into the street.

Going with his gut, Isaac turned his horse towards Edwin. "Who are you?"

Edwin approached and replied, "I'm Edwin Sayer. I work for Mr. Corrigan. He's been expecting you."

"I'm..." Isaac said dismounting his horse.

"Well, isn't that nice, Sheriff. You have a welcoming party. I, on the other hand, don't," Connor said, interrupting Isaac and trotting up next to him.

Isaac cut Connor a sharp look and said, "I'm—"

Once more interrupting Isaac, Connor stuck out his hand to Edwin and said, "My name is Connor McCarthy.

Pleasure to make your acquaintance."

"Same. Are you friends, or were you just traveling with the sheriff?" Edwin asked Connor.

Growing agitated that he couldn't get a word out, Isaac spoke louder. "I'm—"

Facing Isaac, Edwin said, "Sheriff, if you'll allow me, I can escort you to Mr. Corrigan's house. You'll be staying there along with his lovely wife, Lucy."

Isaac froze upon hearing Lucy's name.

"Mr. Corrigan made the arrangements. I hope you'll be satisfied with that. He wants to get to know you and explain everything that's been happening here in town. He desperately wants to chart a course with you on how best to address everything," Edwin explained after noticing the peculiar look on Isaac's face.

"I'm to stay at Mr. Corrigan's house with him and his wife?" Isaac asked.

"Yes, sir," Edwin said. "Again, I hope that is satisfactory to you."

Seeing an opportunity to be close to Lucy, Isaac stuck out his hand and said, "It's a pleasure meeting you, Edwin, and I'd be honored to stay with Mr. Corrigan and his wife."

"Great, right this way, Sheriff," Edwin said, pointing towards the Victorian-style house on the hill above them.

"Don't you want to go finish your shave?" Isaac asked.

Edwin wiped his face with a handkerchief and replied, "He hadn't begun to shave when I spotted you. I'll come back later. I know Mr. Corrigan is anxious to meet you."

With a broad smile, Isaac said, "Well, I'm anxious to meet him too."

Edwin nodded and marched off.

Connor smacked Isaac in the shoulder and said, "Why, hello there, Sheriff."

"This goes nowhere," Isaac said, jabbing his index finger into Connor's burly chest.

"As the Lord is my witness, your secret lives and dies with me," Connor said, a twinkle in his eye. Leaning in close, he said, "Good on ya for doing it. I promise you, you'll never regret starting new."

"We shall see...we shall see," Isaac said before walking away.

Watching him go, Connor hollered out, "I'll be seeing you around...Sheriff."

WILKES' OFFICE, BANE, NEVADA

Taking an ashtray into his grip, Quincy hurled it at the wall. It disintegrated into countless shards and chunks of glass upon hitting the wall.

Casually looking at the fragments of glass, Marcus couldn't help feeling that he hated his job and, more importantly, hated his boss, Quincy Wilkes.

"You told me you shot the sheriff," Quincy said.

"I didn't, I said—"

Charging over with fists clenched in anger, Quincy said, "I specifically told you to get the job done. I expected you to do it; this is why I pay you."

"I sent out a qualified team, but it appears they didn't do the job asked," Marcus said.

"It *appears*...it appears? No, Marcus, they didn't. You first tell me the sheriff had been killed, but his body was missing. Now you're standing here telling me he's arrived in town and is currently at Corrigan's house. You've utterly failed me. I couldn't be more disappointed."

"Would you like me to finish the job?" Marcus asked.

"No, I have another idea, but if you ever let me down again, there will be hell to pay," Quincy said, marching back to his desk. Glancing at the glass fragments, he barked, "Get someone in here to clean this up."

"Will there be anything else?" Marcus asked.

Staring out the window, Quincy said, "Yes, I want a meeting set up with the new sheriff."

"How would you like me to handle that?" Marcus asked, seeking clarification.

"Get word to him that I'm having a reception in his honor at my house tomorrow night, say at six o'clock," Quincy replied.

"Anything else?"

"No, leave me," Quincy said, waving him off.

Marcus clenched his jaws tight, turned and strutted towards the door.

"And, Marcus," Quincy called out.

Marcus stopped but didn't turn around.

"Don't let me down this time," Quincy said.

"I'll make sure the sheriff is at your house tomorrow

for the reception," Marcus said and exited the office. After closing the door, he growled under his breath. His hatred for Quincy was growing. It took every ounce of discipline he had to not kill him, but doing so would foil his well-laid-out plans. Seeing a maid in the corner of his eyes, he turned and said, "Mr. Wilkes needs you to go clean up a mess in his office."

She nodded and headed for the office door.

Marcus once more looked at Quincy's office door. A scowl stretched across his face. He put on his wide-brimmed black hat and headed out the door.

CORRIGAN RESIDENCE, BANE, NEVADA

Isaac followed Edwin into Mortimer's house and stood nervously in the foyer. His mind was spinning with what he was now trying to get away with. He knew the risk but needed to see her. He just prayed that the second she laid eyes on him, she wouldn't expose him.

Edwin spun around and said, "Wait here. I'll go inform Mr. Corrigan you're here." Edwin disappeared into an adjacent room.

Isaac looked around the small foyer. His eyes stopped upon seeing a familiar porcelain angel sitting in the center of an ornate doily. He walked over and picked it up. Looking at it closely, his mind went back to when he'd first seen the statue in her house in New York. He wondered what it was doing here. Had she liked it so much that she'd packed and hauled it all this way?

"That was my mother's," Lucy said from the top of

the stairs.

Isaac froze. His back was to her, so she clearly couldn't see it was him.

Lucy descended the stairs, her hand gliding down the banister. "She died just before I moved to Bane. She loved that angel, said it kept watch on all who entered the house."

Isaac remained still, keeping his back to her.

Lucy reached the ground floor and said, "You must be Sheriff Travis. My husband mentioned you were coming to stay with us until you found accommodations in town."

Apprehension gripped Isaac; he now regretted coming and more importantly the fact that he'd assumed the identity of a dead lawman.

Lucy stepped closer to Isaac. "Is everything alright, Sheriff?" she asked, curious as to why he hadn't turned to engage her in conversation.

Isaac placed the statue back on the table, cleared his throat, and turned to face Lucy.

When her eyes cast upon Isaac's face, her first reaction was confusion. Her mind was trying to comprehend how Isaac could be standing in front of her when it was supposed to be Travis.

Stepping up to her quickly, Isaac whispered, "It's me. Please don't say a word, please. Let me first explain, and if…if that explanation falls short, you may do what you wish."

"What are you doing here?" she asked, taking a step back from him.

"Please, Lucy, let me first explain why I'm here and why…"

"And why you're pretending to be Sheriff Travis?" she asked.

"It's a long story, but please give me the time to detail it all to you. I know you'll understand all of it," he said.

Her face turned ashen followed by a weakness in her knees. "I need to sit down."

He rushed to her side and wrapped an arm around her waist to prevent her from collapsing. "Come, sit down here." He took her to a small chair next to the table in the foyer. "Can I get you a glass of water?"

"No, I just need to rest here a bit," she replied. She took several deep breaths then lifted her head to look at Isaac. "What are you doing here?"

"I'm here to see you," he answered.

"You can't be. I mean, you're supposed to be in prison. Did they let you out? Wait, are you now a sheriff?" she said, the tempo of the questions coming rapidly. She was confused to the point of questioning her own sanity. "Is it really you?" She reached out and touched his face.

"It's me," he said.

"Isaac, you're not supposed to be here. You can't be here," she said.

Footfalls came from the other room.

Isaac stepped away from her so as not to seem as if something inappropriate was occurring.

Lucy got to her feet and walked carefully to the foot

of the stairs. She grasped the banister to steady herself.

Mortimer appeared, a broad smile across his face, with Edwin following. Sticking his hand out, Mortimer said, "Sheriff Travis, so good to finally make your acquaintance."

Edwin stood behind Mortimer, his hands and arms crossed pensively in front of him.

Isaac took Mortimer's hand and shook. "Nice to meet you as well."

"How was your trip from Pennsylvania? I pray it was uneventful," Mortimer asked.

Isaac took a second to think about how he'd answer then proceeded. "It was a pleasant trip."

"Through our correspondence and from your reputation, I was sure you'd be...a bigger man, you know, taller, more robust in stature."

Looking down at himself, Isaac said, "I'm sorry if my appearance disappoints."

"On the contrary. It's just that in our mind's eye we get a picture; then when we see the real thing, it can seem distorted."

"I can assure you I'm Sheriff Ethan Travis," Isaac said as he gave a quick glance to Lucy.

Lucy returned his glance with her own.

Mortimer followed his glance and saw Lucy. "My dear, I apologize, I didn't see you standing there." He motioned towards her and said, "Sheriff, this is my lovely wife, Lucy."

"We met before," Isaac said.

"Oh?" Mortimer asked.

"Yes, I came down the stairs and we chatted for a minute or two just before you came into the room," Lucy clarified.

"I see, well, I'm sure you'd like to get cleaned up," Mortimer said, turning to Edwin. "Show our distinguished guest to his room."

"Yes, sir," Edwin said.

"When you're done, would you care to join me in the parlor for a drink before supper? How does five thirty sound? I'd like to go over the situation we've been dealing with in town and see what you'd like to get started with first."

"Sounds good," Isaac said. "Thank you."

"Sir, when I'm done showing the sheriff to his room, I'd like a word with you concerning the smelting operation and the other business from yesterday we were discussing," Edwin said.

"Just meet me in my office," Mortimer replied.

"I can escort the good sheriff to his room so you two can discuss business," Lucy blurted out.

All eyes turned towards her.

"Are you sure?" Mortimer asked.

"It would be my honor," Lucy said.

"Then please do, my dear," Mortimer said. He turned and said, "Come with me, Edwin."

Mortimer and Edwin disappeared into the room next to them.

Isaac stepped up and said, "Are you feeling well?"

"I will be fine. Now follow me," Lucy said. She briskly walked down the hall and turned right into a room near the end of the hallway.

Isaac followed her into the room and closed the door.

Spinning around, Lucy asked, "Why are you here?"

"I needed to see you."

"You were sentenced to twenty years. How is it you're here?" she asked.

Not wanting to lie, he replied, "I was given an opportunity, so I took it. I immediately came west to find you."

"You escaped?"

"Yes."

"Oh, Isaac, why did you come here, why?"

"I needed to know," he said.

"Know what?" she asked, her heart racing.

"Why didn't you ever come to visit me?"

Lucy lowered her head and stared at the floor. Nervous, she chewed on her lower lip with her teeth.

"I deserve to know," he said.

She lifted her head and narrowed her eyes. "I owe you nothing. You were convicted of a crime and sent away. I was supposed to be your wife, and you betrayed me. You owe me an apology, if anything."

"An apology? I didn't do anything. I was set up by your father," Isaac fired back.

She started to pace the room.

"Just tell me that he prevented you from coming to see me," Isaac pleaded.

"I wanted to see you, but Father was insistent that I not go…"

"I knew it," he blared.

"But," she said then paused.

After waiting for her to continue, he asked, "Is there more?"

"I soon came to realize that maybe you had done something, that maybe I didn't really know you."

"We were to be married!" Isaac grunted.

"At first I didn't think you were capable, but shortly afterwards I had other feelings."

"How is that possible? How can you doubt me, doubt my character?" Isaac asked, his face showing how her words were painful to hear.

"On account that I remember hearing you preach about the poor not having access to coal, but the rich did," she replied, her mind racing back to one of his diatribes concerning wealth inequality.

"You think I organized that robbery?" Isaac asked, shocked.

"I admit that…yes, yes, I did think that maybe you could have," Lucy admitted.

Distraught by her confession, Isaac tore himself away and walked to a large window. He stared out towards the west and the valley beyond.

"You can't be here. You need to leave," she said.

Her words stung him again.

"If someone finds out that you escaped and that you're an imposter, they'll hang you," she said.

"Stop pretending you care."

"I do care; truth be told, I never stopped caring. I just…I just couldn't convince my father to let me come visit you. Even though I had those doubts, I still cared, I still thought of you," she said, her tone softer. "I *still* think of you."

He turned around and looked into her green eyes. "Those four long years I spent in prison, there wasn't a day that went by that I didn't think of you. I suspected your father kept you away, but to hear you say now that you could imagine me committing such an act is hurtful. I never did anything wrong except want to marry you."

"You think that was wrong?" she asked, tears forming in her eyes.

"Our love wasn't wrong, that's not what I'm trying to say. It was your father, that's what was wrong. I didn't think he'd stoop to the level he did to stop it. I misjudged him," Isaac said, taking a step closer to her.

She wiped the forming tears from her eyes and said, "You need to leave. Please go."

"Come with me," Isaac pleaded, stepping forward and taking her hands.

She didn't resist his touch.

"We can leave now, saddle up some horses and ride, just you and me. Lucy, we can finally be together," he said.

She didn't say a word.

"Please come with me," Isaac urged.

Pulling her hands away from his, she said, "I can't. I'm married now. What sort of life would I…we have? You're an escaped convict, and I'd be an adulterous wife. Where would we go?"

"We could go anywhere. Board a ship in San

Francisco and go to South America, maybe the Orient or even Australia."

"We don't have anything, no money, no status," she said.

"We can make it. I just want you above all else."

Hearing Mortimer call out further in the house, she hastily stepped away from Isaac and rushed to the door. Before turning the knob, she looked over her shoulder and said, "Leave while you can. Please, before someone finds out you're not who you say you are."

"I won't leave Bane unless you're with me," Isaac said.

"I can't, I won't go with you. My life is now with Mortimer. He's a good man, a good husband. This is my fate now," she said, turning the knob. She opened the door fully and left.

Isaac opened his mouth to rebut her last comment, but the door closed before he could form his words. Lucy stood in the hallway just outside the bedroom. She again wiped tears from her eyes.

"Lucy, where are you?" Mortimer cried out from the parlor.

She stepped to a mirror in the hall and glanced at her reflection. She fixed her hair and smoothed out her dress.

"Lucy?" Mortimer again called out.

"I'll be right there," she replied loudly.

"Hurry, please," he said.

Taking a deep breath and exhaling, she said, "Stop thinking about it. There's no future with Isaac, it's over."

The bedroom door cracked open and Isaac peered

out.

Catching him looking at her in the reflection in the mirror, Lucy turned and sped off down the hallway.

Isaac opened the door further and watched until she went into the parlor. "I'm not leaving, Lucy Mae...not without you."

***

Mortimer brought Edwin into his office. "Take a seat."

Edwin did as he was told. "Sir, we're beginning to rebuild the barn."

"Let's skip that. Tell me who this source is," Mortimer said, sitting on the edge of his desk and looking down with firm eyes on Edwin.

Clenching his hands and chewing on his lower lip, Edwin stuttered, "Sir, um, I don't feel comfortable disclosing that just yet."

"Edwin, we discussed who you worked for yesterday."

"Yes, sir."

"I expect you to tell me who this mystery person is, and do it now," Mortimer said sternly.

"Sir, can I just reveal who he works for and keep it at that?"

"Let's begin there," Mortimer said.

"He works for Mr. Wilkes. He doesn't like the man and wishes to help you, but he requested he remain anonymous for fear of reprisal."

"Can he confirm if Wilkes is behind the silver

robbery?"

"He's not confirmed that, sir. So it appears it was someone else," Edwin said.

Mortimer looked away and thought. It was good that he was receiving information from inside Wilkes' operation, but he wondered if it was true or not.

"I've got a couple of men doing some due diligence on the parcel of land. I'm attempting to get a separate opinion on its viability. I thought it best versus just taking my source's word for it."

"Good, do that. Better to know. And who owns it?"

"Oh, yes, I forgot. It's owned by a man named Wilfred Scott. He resides in Placerville, California."

"Find out who he is if you can," Mortimer ordered.

"Yes, sir."

"You can go," Mortimer said.

"Do you want to discuss the barn?"

"No, and, Edwin, I expect you to tell me who this source is at a later date when you feel it can be revealed without jeopardizing him," Mortimer said.

Hopping up quickly, Edwin replied, "Yes, sir." He rushed to the door and left.

***

Isaac cleaned up and changed his clothes. It felt good to take a bath, it not only washed away the days of dust and sweat, but it soothed his achy muscles.

He exited the bedroom but found the hallway and beyond empty. He made his way to the parlor to find it also void of anyone. He pulled out his pocket watch to check the time; it was five twenty-eight.

The parlor was ornately decorated. If he hadn't ridden into town, he could be mistaken that he was in a house in New York. The windows were adorned with thick burgundy curtains; golden tassels dangled from the edges. Built-in bookcases spanned the far walls, the shelves full from end to end with books. Opposite that was a fireplace; above on the mantel sat a clock, and above that a portrait of someone he didn't know. Two wing-back chairs sat facing the fire with a small round table in between; on that a pipe and tobacco box sat waiting for their user to enjoy. In the center of the room two tufted couches faced each other; only an oval coffee table separated them.

Curious as to the expansive book collection, Isaac made his way to the bookcases and began to examine the spines. He spotted *Moby-Dick* by Herman Melville. He pulled it out and opened the hardbound cover. Inside was an inscription on the title page made out to Mortimer by Melville himself.

"I so enjoyed that book," Mortimer said, entering the room.

Startled, Isaac quickly closed the book and placed it back on the shelf.

"If you haven't read it, I encourage you to," Mortimer said, removing the book and offering it to Isaac.

"It's fine, I've read it before," Isaac said. "I was merely looking at it. The book brings me back to the war."

"This book?" Mortimer asked, curious as to the meaning of what he just said.

"I read it during the war," Isaac answered.

Placing the book back on the shelf, Mortimer said, "I can imagine losing the war was tough on you."

"Losing?" Isaac asked, confused by the comment.

Making his way to a liquor cart, Mortimer pulled out a bottle of brandy and said, "I didn't get the opportunity to fight, but I do remember quite clearly the Confederacy lost."

Jolted back to his false identity, Isaac replied, "I was meaning that in the heart of us rebels, we never truly lost, and there are some who say the South will rise again."

"Brandy?" Mortimer asked.

Feeling he needed to stay in character, Isaac said, "Brandy is fine, but us Texans prefer whiskey."

"I have that as well," Mortimer said, taking a decanter of whiskey and pouring a glass half full. He handed it to Isaac and said, "Let's sit and talk."

The two men sat in the wing-back chairs.

Mortimer stared at the crackling fire and composed his thoughts while Isaac ran through all the information he'd gleamed from Travis in the short time he'd known him.

"For a Texan, you don't have much of an accent," Mortimer said.

"I suppose my time in Pennsylvania rubbed off on me," Isaac replied.

"If you're hiding it for fear of how I'd respond, it's

fine. I can imagine when you worked in Pennsylvania, some didn't take too kindly to a rebel being their head law enforcement officer."

"I found the Yankee hospitality quite warm, actually," Isaac said.

"Good, we're not as bad as old Jefferson Davis made us out to be," Mortimer joked, referencing the old Confederate president.

"Sheriff, do you mind if I just jump right into the business at hand?" Mortimer asked.

"Please do."

Mortimer shifted in his chair so he could face Isaac. "Mining towns are known to be rowdy places, but what I'm dealing with now has the potential to ruin me. As I stipulated in my letter to you, there is someone here trying to sabotage what I've built here. They have caused great harm by attempting to get the miners to organize, causing delays; but the most egregious thing has just occurred. A shipment of silver was hijacked and stolen; then a day later our smelting operation was destroyed. I can deal with the rowdiness in town, but the other attacks and the disruption of our mining operations could cost me the much-needed financing I need to expand. You see, I have an investor coming soon, and I'll put it this way, he has become a man who is very risk averse. If he discovers I have a problem here that makes this mining operation vulnerable, he won't invest."

"What happened to the last sheriff?"

Mortimer cocked his head and gave Isaac an odd look. "He was murdered. Do you not recall that from my letter?"

"I apologize, I must have forgotten that small detail," Isaac said.

"It's not a small detail. Having the sheriff murdered is no small detail," Mortimer said. "Then as you'll recall in my letter, the other sheriff was bribed, by whom I still don't know. You see, Sheriff Travis, I need a tough lawman like yourself to come in here and straighten things out. I've been made aware that your tactics could possibly backfire as it pertains to some of the townspeople, but right now I can live with that. I need you to find this saboteur and shut them down using any means necessary."

"You mean kill them?" Isaac asked before taking a sip of whiskey.

Leaning in close to Isaac, Mortimer said, "Sheriff, I hired you because of your reputation. I think you know what I mean."

"I do," Isaac said, his mind now contemplating the greater problem at hand for him. "Do you have anyone that you suspect?"

"I do. There's a small-time bar owner and businessman here named Quincy Wilkes. I've heard rumors he's behind it, but I don't have enough to move against him."

"You own this town, don't you?" Isaac asked rhetorically.

"Yes."

"Then revoke his leases or raise his fees. There must be something you can do to leverage him," Isaac said.

"I've thought about that, believe me; but if I were to do so without evidence of any kind, it could make for a very bad situation with the other business owners who have come here. You see, Sheriff, I plan on expanding my operations. If I have a reputation for spiteful acts with nothing solid to back it up, I could suffer. While I own this town, I don't own everything in it, and I don't run it like a dictator. I want the people to come and go as they please; however…" Mortimer said, pausing.

"However?" Isaac asked.

"I want you to be on that man and investigate. If you find it's him, I want him and whoever is working with him dealt with harshly."

"You've got the right man," Isaac said, playing the role again with his bravado talk.

"I also need you to work fast. My investor is to arrive in a week's time; he's just boarded a train in New York. I need this trouble finalized before he arrives."

"I'll get it done, I can assure you," Isaac said in a confident tone though he had no idea just how he'd do it.

Mortimer tossed his brandy back in one gulp, stood and headed for the liquor cart. "I knew I got the right man. Enjoy tonight; then start first thing in the morning. Your men will be waiting for you at the sheriff's office. As far as your accommodations, I think it's best you stay here until this trouble is past. I don't need you murdered in your sleep like the one sheriff was."

"How many men do I have?" Isaac asked.

"As many as you need. If you want an army, then hire one. I'll spare no expense," Mortimer said, pouring himself another glass of brandy.

"Good."

Mortimer drank some brandy and said, "I know the compensation I'm paying you is generous, but I'm a believer in truly motivating people. We all work for money, and the more money available to be made will make a man work harder. If you get this handled before Mr. Wagner arrives, I'll give you a bonus of one thousand dollars."

Hearing the name Mr. Wagner sent a shiver down Isaac's spine.

Seeing Isaac's peculiar look, Mortimer said, "Is that too low? How about fifteen hundred?"

"That's fine, fifteen hundred is perfectly fine, thank you," Isaac said, wondering if the Mr. Wagner he mentioned was Lucy's father.

"This Mr. Wagner you have coming to town, we should provide safe passage for him. I'll send a team to meet him in Elko upon his arrival. What day will that be?"

"He arrives in Elko on November 2, early. I want to have him here by the third," Mortimer replied. "As far as the security escort, you think that's wise? Won't that signal that we have troubles here?" Mortimer asked.

"I think you should send your own coach instead of having him take a commercial one. That way you can have my men guarding him."

"I see your approach, let's not stick him with the general public on the coach," Mortimer said.

"Correct," Isaac said. "Is this Mr. Wagner the well-known businessman from New York?"

"It is, and he's also my father-in-law," Mortimer replied.

Isaac gulped upon hearing the confirmation of who was coming. He so far had convinced Lucy not to divulge his true identity, but he knew without a doubt he wouldn't be so lucky with Everett.

Phyllis entered the room and said, "Mr. Corrigan, dinner is now ready."

"Great, thank you, Phyllis," Mortimer said.

Phyllis exited as quickly as she had appeared.

Turning to Isaac, Mortimer said, "I hope you brought your appetite. Phyllis makes wonderful food."

"I'm very hungry, I look forward to it and, Mr. Corrigan..."

Interrupting Isaac, Mortimer said, "Call me Mortimer."

"Mortimer, thank you for the opportunity and thank you for the hospitality."

"You're quite welcome. And, Sheriff," Mortimer said.

Now standing with his empty glass in his hand, Isaac said, "Yes."

"If anyone approaches you, wants to pay you off, please know that I'll match it and then some. Know that I'll do what's necessary for your financial well-being so that you don't have to go anywhere else."

"You want me to tell you if someone's trying to buy me off," Isaac said.

"Yes."

"I work exclusively for you, no one else, and if someone does approach me, you'll be the next to know about it."

"Good man. Come, let's dine," Mortimer said, patting Isaac on the shoulder.

The two exited the room and stepped across the hallway and into the dining room. Two large candelabras helped illuminate the space, along with four wall-mounted candle sconces. The bright orange glow provided more than adequate light.

Mortimer took a seat at the head of the table and motioned with his hand to a chair to his right. "Please, sit."

Isaac did as he said. Curious as to where Lucy was, he asked, "Will your wife be joining us for dinner?"

"I'm afraid not. She's not feeling well. She's been getting these bad migraines since we arrived in Bane. Poor thing struggles to be well. She's never been the healthiest; even when I first met her, she struggled."

"I'm sorry to hear that she won't be joining us and that she has a chronic condition. Has a doctor seen her?" Isaac asked, genuinely concerned for Lucy.

"Yes, I had a doctor brought in from Carson City. He thinks it's anxiety, so he prescribed her laudanum."

Knowing the addictive traits of that drug, Isaac said, "I've heard some negative things about laudanum. I'd reconsider if I were you."

Phyllis came into the room and served a slice of roast to each of their plates then generously covered it with gravy.

Both men thanked her.

She nodded and departed the room.

"Please, enjoy," Mortimer said, a knife and fork in his hands.

Isaac leaned ever so closer to the plate and took in the rich aroma of the food. It had been a long time since he'd enjoyed a meal like this.

"Tell me about your time in the war," Mortimer said.

Chewing his food, Isaac waited to reply.

"I'd also enjoy hearing about your exploits as a Texas Ranger," Mortimer said with a broad smile.

Wiping his mouth with a napkin, Isaac said, "If you don't mind, I'd rather not discuss my times in the war or my days as a Ranger."

"Oh," Mortimer said, a somber and disappointed look on his face.

"I'm not trying to be difficult, it was just a tough time for me," Isaac said, answering the question honestly. He found he disliked talking about his own time in the war to those who hadn't fought. They'd usually nod and pat him on the back, then offer congratulations for winning as if he alone had brought the Confederacy to its knees. Of course, there was the rarer response, like that of Everett, who looked upon him as a killer or warmonger. Either way, if his time ever was brought up, he'd acknowledge he'd served then keep it at that.

The two men continued their meal, both exchanging pleasantries and idle chat. It was something that Mortimer found disappointing, but for Isaac he was quite content to keep it that way.

With dinner over, Isaac stood and said, "I'm going to retire. I've had a long trip, and I have a big day tomorrow."

"You sure you won't join me in the parlor for another drink?" Mortimer asked.

"I'm sure," Isaac said.

"Goodnight then, Sheriff," Mortimer said.

"Goodnight," Isaac replied.

Before Isaac could depart, Mortimer said, "One more thing, Deputy Wallace seems to be a good and decent man, trustworthy."

"And the others?" Isaac asked.

"The others are all new hires," Mortimer said.

"What happened to the others?" Isaac asked.

"All killed."

"Good to know," Isaac said. He promptly departed the dining room and hurried down the hall. As he passed the stairwell, he glanced up with hopes of spotting Lucy, but she wasn't there. He was troubled by her illness and questioned what the source of her ailment was. Could it be that she was suffering from heartache? Could she be telling him the truth that she never stopped loving him? Was her marriage to Mortimer one born of convenience? If it was, their relationship was still salvageable. A smile broke out across his face as that thought sank deeper, giving him hope that they could still have a future together.

CHAPTER SIX

OCTOBER 30, 1869

SHERIFF'S OFFICE, BANE, NEVADA

Isaac woke early. He had a big day today, as it was his first day on the job as a sheriff. Never having been a lawman, he had some uneasiness about having the ability to do the job and not look as if he wasn't who he said he was.

He made his way to the sheriff's office under Edwin's guidance. Inside, he found the office occupied with longing faces, no doubt his deputies. One man jumped up and came towards him.

"I'm Deputy Wallace. It's a pleasure to meet you," Wallace said, his arm extended, a jovial look upon his stubbled face.

Isaac took his hand and shook. "Nice meeting you too."

"Let me be the first to welcome you to the Bane Sheriff's office. Oh, I should introduce you to your deputies," Wallace said.

"Very well," Isaac said.

"From the left you have Jess—that's short for Jessie—Ernie, Bill, Porter and Wesley."

The men all gave him their own unique salutations.

"Nice to make your acquaintance. As you know, we have a big job ahead of us. Wallace, I heard you're the most senior man here. Can you fill me in on what I should know?"

"Sure thing, Sheriff," Wallace replied happily.

Wallace detailed the information they knew regarding the fire at the smelter and the silver shipment being hijacked, though he offered no relevant details of who might be behind either.

The door of the office opened.

All turned their heads to see Marcus walk in.

"I'm looking for the new sheriff," Marcus said.

Isaac sized him up and said, "That'll be me. Who's asking?"

Marcus stepped up to Isaac and said, "Mr. Wilkes wishes to convey an invitation for you to join him at his residence tonight for a reception in your honor."

Recalling the name, Isaac asked, "Mr. Wilkes is having a reception for me? Why?"

Ignoring any of Isaac's questions, Marcus continued. "The reception begins at six. He insists on you coming."

"He insists?" Isaac asked, finding a bit of humor in Marcus' tough-man approach.

"I'll relay to him to expect you," Marcus said.

"Hold on, I didn't say I was going," Isaac said.

"Mr. Wilkes insists," Marcus said.

"That's well and good, but I don't know who Mr. Wilkes is, nor do I just do what someone tells me to do."

Knowing if he returned without having confirmation from Isaac, Marcus said, "It would behoove you to attend this reception in your honor."

"And why's that?" Isaac asked, his arms folded in

front of him.

"Mr. Wilkes is a rich and influential man; you don't want to be on his bad side," Marcus said.

Isaac thought about the situation and came to the conclusion that attending the reception could be beneficial. It would allow him to possibly identify if Quincy was the saboteur.

"What's your answer?" Marcus asked.

"Tell Mr. Wilkes I'll be there, though I may be late," Isaac said.

Marcus didn't utter another word; he pivoted as if on a dime and exited the office.

Wallace stepped up to Isaac and whispered, "Some say Mr. Wilkes is the man behind everything. Some say he was even the man who bribed the last sheriff."

"Deputy, my intention on going to this event is to gather information. I'm not attending to receive a bribe. I can assure you I'm here to catch whoever has taken that silver shipment and whoever destroyed that smelting operation."

"Good," Wallace said.

"I almost forgot, Mr. Corrigan has an important guest arriving on the train in Elko on November 2. Send a private coach with a team to provide security all the way back to town," Isaac ordered.

"How many men?" Wallace asked.

"Two should be sufficient, and make sure they are presentable, and tell them not to discuss the troubles in town with him," Isaac said.

"Who is it?" Wallace asked.

"Mr. Wagner, he's Mrs. Corrigan's father," Isaac answered, his stomach turning just at the mere mention of his name.

"I'll get right on it," Wallace said.

Isaac turned to the others and said with a raised voice, "Let's cover some of my ground rules."

WILKES' OFFICE, BANE, NEVADA

Marcus immediately reported to Quincy to give him the news of Isaac coming to the event, but was told to wait outside.

Fifteen minutes passed and still he waited.

Quincy's office door opened, and out stepped Duncan McCarthy, Connor's brother and owner of McCarthy Livery and Stables.

Marcus gave him a curious look. He sped out of the front office space and exited quickly out the door.

"Get in here!" Quincy hollered.

Marcus got to his feet and went inside the office. Curious as to Duncan's appearance, he asked, "What's the Scotsman doing here?"

Lifting his head from a set of papers, Quincy answered bluntly, "That's none of your business."

Marcus gritted his teeth.

"Do you have something to tell me?" Quincy asked.

"Yes, the new sheriff confirms he will be attending tonight."

"How does he look?" Quincy asked.

"Look?"

"Is he an imposing man? His stature, I'm asking about his stature," Quincy said.

"He's tall, not too tall, looks a bit skinny, if you ask me," Marcus said.

"I hear he has a reputation, one for being tough as nails. We need to watch everything we do until after I get a chance to talk with him tonight. If all goes well, he'll be working for me by the end of the day. If not, then we'll have to figure out something else if he gets in our way," Quincy said.

"I understand," Marcus said.

"Have you found my silver?" Quincy asked concerning the silver shipment they'd stolen having also been stolen.

"No."

"How well are you looking?" Quincy asked.

"I'm limited in manpower right now, but I will do my best to have it tracked down. I've sent a team to Elko and other depots, including Carson City."

"I need that silver," Quincy barked.

"I understand," Marcus simply replied.

"How come you never call me sir? Hmm? You don't show me any respect. I'm your boss; I pay you well."

Like he often did, Marcus ignored questions he didn't want to answer. "If there's anything else?"

Quincy hopped to his feet and walked over to Marcus. "Do I need to hire someone new to handle your responsibilities?"

"No."

"I can't stress it enough, I need that silver found and

found fast. I'm out on a ledge here," Quincy said.

"We're looking, and I will do my best."

"Stop saying that. I need you to find it; I need a guarantee."

Growing weary, Marcus sniped, "I can't give a guarantee. There's hundreds of square miles to search, but I will do what I can within my power."

Quincy seethed at the response.

"Is that all?" Marcus asked.

"Yes, now get out of here," Quincy barked.

Marcus turned and exited.

Quincy paced the office a few times before sitting back down. If he couldn't find that silver, he'd most likely lose his chance to acquire the parcel of land and put down his share in the mining company he desperately wanted to start with the investors he had coming to town. However, he did have one other option, one he didn't like, as it was risky and could put all his enterprises in jeopardy and him perilously close to financial ruin. If the first came and he didn't have the silver, he'd make that decision then.

MCCARTHY LIVERY AND STABLES, BANE, NEVADA

Connor tossed a saddle over a beam and with a snorty tone said, "I didn't expect to see you anytime soon, Sheriff." When he said sheriff, he did so emphasizing it above the other words.

Isaac rolled his eyes and said, "I don't know who to

talk to, so I came to see you."

Connor walked up to Isaac, patted his shoulder, and said, "Do you find it a blessing or a curse that your sole friend is an ex-convict from Scotland?"

Ignoring his smart-ass comment, Isaac continued, "I saw her, and she looks no different, really, since I saw her last."

"And that was how long ago?"

"Four years ago."

"Being that you're here, I reckon she didn't reveal your secret."

"She told me to leave town. She's concerned for me, and rightly so, I'm risking everything," Isaac said.

"My friend, you sound like a boy with all this talk. Leave the poor woman be. What exactly are you thinking will come from this? Huh? She's married to the man who owns the damn town. If he wanted to, he could squash you with the plentiful sacks of gold that he owns."

"He'd probably use silver," Isaac joked.

Connor smiled, wagged his finger at Isaac, and said, "That, my friend, was funny."

"You know why I came here."

"Yes, you said you needed to ask her a question. So did ya? Did you ask your question?"

"Yes."

"Now it's time to leave or move on; you've accomplished what you came here to do. Stop this nonsense before it costs you your damn life," Connor said sincerely.

"I think she still loves me," Isaac said.

"Love, feelings, blah, blah, blah. Listen, friend, you can't have her; that moment in time has come and gone. You're living in the past. I know what happened to you was wrong, though I still don't know what that was specifically, but it was wrong. Life isn't easy, there aren't guarantees, life isn't fair. Life is life; it's suffering layered with fleeting moments of bliss and drunkenness and an occasional lass to lay with. Stop acting like you deserve this woman, 'cause you don't."

"Connor, if you're done running your jib, I could use you at the front. I need you to open the side barn. We've got to store a wagon for a customer," Duncan, Connor's brother, hollered. Duncan not only rented out and sheltered horses, but also had a barn open for storage of about anything that could fit in there, for a fee.

Connor placed his hand on Isaac's shoulder and squeezed. "I know you think I carry on and that I don't take life seriously. The thing is, I do; hence why I try to enjoy it and have fun as much as I can. I suggest you do the same before you end up behind bars again or, worse, hanging from the gallows."

Isaac thought about everything Connor said, and he listened to it with an open mind. Connor did convey wisdom and truths that resonated, but something stirred in him that he needed to explore. The one thing that Connor mentioned was this feeling of deserving Lucy. He did feel that way, and it all stemmed from him thinking he'd been cheated of a life with her. He hated to lose, and if he had a chance, though slim, he'd try to make a win out of this after all.

WILKES RESIDENCE, BANE, NEVADA

Before Isaac departed for the reception, he informed Mortimer of the event. Like him, Mortimer thought it was a good idea.

Wearing a new suit he'd purchased along the train ride out to Elko and making sure he wore Travis' gun belt with the Remington holstered, he arrived at Quincy's front door.

The door opened with Marcus on the other side of the threshold. "Sheriff, Mr. Wilkes is expecting you."

Isaac stepped in and asked, "Do you ever smile?"

"He's down the hall in the den," Marcus said, motioning with his hand.

Looking around, Isaac saw a handful of people gathered, enjoying drinks and mingling. He made his way into the den and scanned the faces.

"Sheriff Travis!" Quincy howled happily.

"You must be Mr. Wilkes?" Isaac asked.

"That I am, and I can tell you, it's not always fun being me," Quincy joked. "So have you settled in nicely?"

"I have."

"Rumor says you're staying with Mr. Corrigan, is that true?"

"It is, he's a most generous man," Isaac said. "I have to ask why this event for me?"

"I'm known for my generosity as it pertains to these sorts of things. I believe everyone of importance who is new to town should be welcomed with open arms."

"That's mighty civil," Isaac said. "Tell me, what's your business in town?"

"The question should be, what's not my business in town?" Quincy laughed.

"So you're involved in many things?" Isaac asked.

"Yes, sir, I am. I like to keep my investments diverse, as they say." Quincy chuckled.

"I suppose that's smart. I for one am not keen on business. That's why I went into law enforcement," Isaac said.

"Word is you're from Texas. I don't hear a twang," Quincy said.

"It comes after I've had a few drinks," Isaac lied.

Looking at Isaac's empty hand, Quincy's eyes widened. "Get this man a drink. I didn't notice until just now that you didn't have one. I so apologize. You're the man being honored, and you don't even have a drink to toast if we had one." Quincy waved over a servant.

The servant handed Isaac a whiskey.

"Will that do?" Quincy asked.

Taking the whiskey, Isaac replied, "It will. I've got a question, this might seem out of place, but how come Mr. Corrigan wasn't invited?"

Leaning in close so as not to be overheard, Quincy answered, "On account that he and I don't see eye to eye on many things."

"You don't get along?"

"That's the polite way of saying it," Quincy said.

"Have you done something to cause this fracture or strain in your relationship?" Isaac asked.

Quincy scoffed and said, "You'll soon come to find that Mr. Corrigan doesn't know what he's doing. It's his incompetence that has caused issues between us due to the fact I call him on the carpet on such things."

Marcus stepped up to Quincy, leaned in, and whispered something in his ear.

Quincy's eyes widened like saucers. He whispered something back to Marcus, who turned and walked off.

"Is everything okay?" Isaac asked.

"Everything is fine, and when it's not, it usually gets sorted out rather quickly," Quincy answered. "Come, let me introduce you to other business owners in town."

Taking care and diligence, Quincy walked Isaac around the party, introducing him to everyone there. It was very helpful for Isaac; it enabled him to have a crash course on the who's who in town. One thing he suspected was coming was the bribe, he knew it would come soon, so he patiently waited.

***

After dinner, and a subsequent toast to the new sheriff, the party went back to the den to continue drinking and to gamble.

"Do you gamble?" Quincy asked Isaac.

"Every day," Isaac replied.

"Is poker your game?"

"Life is," Isaac answered.

"Ha, I suppose as a lawman, you do gamble with your life daily. It's too bad you don't make the money that's equal to the effort or risk," Quincy said.

And right there, Isaac knew the bribe was coming.

"Sheriff Travis, if you have a moment, care to join me in my personal office for a cigar?" Quincy asked.

"Sure."

The two left the den and marched to the office down the hall. Once inside, Quincy closed the double pocket doors and headed for a wooden box, which sat on the corner of his desk. He pulled out two cigars, handed one to Isaac, and said, "I have them brought in from San Francisco. They're from the Dominican Republic."

Isaac held the unlit cigar to his nose; the rich aroma of the cigar smelled good. "I don't think I've ever had a cigar from there."

"You'll enjoy it," Quincy said, offering Isaac a cutter and matches.

It had been a while since Isaac had smoked a cigar, but he recalled how to prepare a cigar to smoke. He cut off the butt end and lit a match. He placed it under the tip and began to inhale. The flame danced around as it lit the end. Isaac kept inhaling in puffs until the entire end lit orange with each inhale. As the smoke swirled across his tongue, he was transported back to one of the last cigars he'd smoked. It was the day the war ended; Gerald had visited and brought with him a box of cigars, a bottle of whiskey, and a copy of the *New York Herald* newspaper, the headline reading LEE SURRENDERS, THE WAR IS OVER!

"Sheriff?" Quincy asked.

Snapping out of his daydream, Isaac said, "Sorry, I

was lost deep in thought."

"I could see that," Quincy said. "Have a seat. There's something I wish to discuss."

The two men sat down, Isaac in an armed chair across from Quincy, who plopped into a large heavy upholstered chair.

"I want us to be friends," Quincy said.

"So do I," Isaac said.

"I have many resources in town, a lot of men working for me. If you ever are in need of assistance, please don't hesitate to ask."

"Okay, I like that. Can I ask for some help now?" Isaac asked.

Quincy sat up, his interest piqued. "Of course, anything."

"Who stole the silver shipment?"

"I don't know, but I have had my men looking into it since the sheriff's office is undermanned," Quincy said. "If I discover anything, I'll be sure to let you know."

"What about the smelter?"

"Same answer. I just don't know who would do such a thing. We need that smelter for the town's success, and if the town is successful, then we all are."

"So all of your resources haven't heard anything?" Isaac asked.

"Nothing."

"Fair enough," Isaac said.

"If I help you, could you possibly be available to help me?" Quincy asked.

"Help? In what capacity could I help you?" Isaac

asked.

"All I'm saying, Sheriff, is if I help, are you willing to help me or my businesses if ever the need should arise."

"That depends, Mr. Wilkes."

"On what?" Quincy asked.

"On what you're asking me to help you with. I'm not one who likes to be indebted to anyone," Isaac replied.

"Sheriff Travis, I'm only saying that we should help each other. The world is a tough place. Life is easier when you have friends," Quincy said.

"Is that all you're offering for my help?" Isaac asked, hoping to lead him.

"Sheriff Travis, I would never presume to offer a man of the law money in exchange for favors," Quincy answered.

"Good, because I'd hate to embarrass you by turning down any offers. Listen, Mr. Wilkes, if you can help, I'll always accept, but I'll never make a blanket agreement. If you want to help me, you're helping the town. I imagine you'd want to do that because you're a generous man."

Quincy gave Isaac a toothy grin and said, "Good chat. How about we go back to your party?"

"Good idea, and thank you for the whiskey," Isaac said, getting up.

The two went back to the party and never mentioned anything of their conversation again.

CORRIGAN RESIDENCE, BANE, NEVADA

Isaac entered the darkened house. The only light he saw

was coming from the parlor. It could be a candle or even the coals of the fireplace. He gently closed the door and slowly walked down the hall, hoping he wouldn't wake anyone.

As he passed the parlor, he glanced inside but didn't see anyone. Thankful that he wouldn't have to discuss his evening, he proceeded towards his bedroom.

"Sheriff Travis?" Mortimer asked from the parlor.

Isaac stopped. He gritted his teeth and stepped back towards the parlor. He poked his head in and said, "Good evening."

"Please come sit. I wish to hear how the party went," Mortimer said.

Isaac came into the room and walked to the wingback chairs. There he found Mortimer slouched in the chair, a half-empty glass in his hand.

"Sit, please," Mortimer said.

Isaac did as he requested.

"So how was Mr. Wilkes?" Mortimer asked, his speech slurring a bit.

"Going was valuable. I learned a lot."

"Like what? Do tell."

"It's evident you and Mr. Wilkes don't have a good relationship. Also he offered me a deal—"

"He did? He tried to bribe you?" Mortimer asked, sitting up erect.

"No, he didn't bribe me. What he asked for was to exchange favors," Isaac said.

"No bribes? He didn't try to pay you to work for him?" Mortimer asked, his tone sounding disappointed.

"You sound upset," Isaac said.

"I thought he'd attempt to bribe you. I thought we had him," Mortimer said.

"He's feeling me out. Give him time; he'll try again," Isaac said before yawning.

"You should go get some rest," Mortimer said.

"I wanted to tell you that I'm hiring another twenty deputies," Isaac said.

"That many?"

"I have plans for them all. I'm sending a team out to track down the stolen silver. I also need some to escort all shipments through the pass. I'm also doubling our presence on the streets."

Mortimer smiled.

"I have an early day tomorrow," Isaac said, getting to his feet.

"Sheriff?" Mortimer asked.

"Yes," Isaac said.

Mortimer paused. He looked at the glass in his hand as he swirled the brandy. "I never told you how I got this town."

"No. No, you didn't," Isaac said, not really caring to know. However, he knew he needed to give Mortimer the attention he wanted.

"I'm always one to look for opportunities. I was at a cocktail party in New York. This man—he was highly intoxicated, by the way—made a fool of himself. Anyway, he was a friend of a friend, that sort of thing. He said he owned a town and a silver-mining company. I was immediately intrigued. As the night went on and the drunker he got, he told me everything about this town, said it produced a ton of silver every two weeks. He was incredibly proud, and I would be too. I was jealous, immensely jealous. I kept thinking how does a man own a town? Later on I saw him at the poker table. He was playing badly, very badly. He ran out of money; the house wouldn't lend him any on account they didn't know him. So I vouched. He was given more but proceeded to lose it quickly. He again asked for more money. The house told him no. He was furious. He felt he could win but just needed more money to do so. Again he came to me; somehow he thought we had rapport, probably because I asked him a lot of questions. People like to talk and be the center of attention," Mortimer said. He took a drink from his glass and continued. "I told him that I would forward him the money, but he needed to play me. He was shocked by my request but accepted. I gave him the money, and we played and played and played. Before I knew it, the sun was rising and he was in debt to me for seventy thousand."

"Seventy thousand?" Isaac asked, shocked by the amount.

"I told you his town did well. So here we are at the table, I raised him more than he had, he asked me for another loan, and I told him no. You should have seen him; his face turned the brightest red. I then told him that if he wanted to stay in the game, he needed to put his town on the table. At first he refused, but before he left the table, he said he would. I suppose he felt his hand was strong, which I knew it wasn't. When he put down his hand, he thought he had it won; then he saw mine, full house, aces high. He exploded, tossed the table, and proceeded to threaten my life. He accused me of cheating, which promptly resulted him being tossed out. The irony was, I had cheated…I cheated from the first hand, I saw a weakness in him, and I was going to exploit it. I broke him and took the town. A week afterwards I felt so bad about it, I went to see him and gave him money," Mortimer said, laughing. "I felt sorry that I'd cheated him. Now you're standing in the house that was his in the town that he once owned. The moral of the story is that every man has a weakness. Find Wilkes' weakness and exploit it, Sheriff."

"You sorta stole this town," Isaac said, a feeling of disgust in his stomach.

"I didn't steal it; he gave it away. There's a difference. He should have had more discipline than that," Mortimer said, defending himself.

"Does your wife know how you acquired the town?" Isaac asked.

"No, she doesn't need to know, nor do I bother to tell her the details. The fairer sex needn't be concerned with the affairs of men," Mortimer said.

"Interesting story," Isaac said.

"Remember the moral of it—every man has a weakness," Mortimer said, tipping his glass.

"I'll keep that in mind, good night," Isaac said.

"Good first day. Go get some rest. I'll see you tomorrow," Mortimer said.

"Oh, how's Mrs. Corrigan? Is she feeling better?"

Isaac asked.

"She is better, thank you for asking. She wanted to know if you'll be available to have dinner with us tomorrow. I told her I wasn't sure if you were," Mortimer said.

"I'll be here," Isaac said. "Good evening, Mortimer."

"Good evening, Sheriff."

Isaac went to his room, closed the door and washed up. When he pulled the quilt back on the bed, a piece of paper fell on the floor. He picked it up, unfolded it, and began to read. It was from Lucy.

Dear Isaac,

Please know that I still care. I have suffered four long years without you. It would be a lie to say I don't still love you, but think of it now as love that can never be conjoined. No matter how my heart aches for us to be together, I've come to the realization that it will never be. There was something I never told you: my father is coming to Bane. He is set to arrive on November 3rd. Once he sees you, you'll be arrested or, worse, hanged. I implore you to leave. Leave this town. Go do what I can't do, get out, live your life, and find love elsewhere. I am lost to you now.

Lucy

Isaac folded the note and set it on the nightstand. A crushing emotional wave crashed over him. He sat on the bed and stared at the paper in his hand. She had admitted the night before that she still cared for him, and now she stated she loved him. He reread the note. This time he came away with the sentiment that she wasn't being selfless, but crying out for help. She was trapped and she needed him to save her.

CHAPTER SEVEN

OCTOBER 31, 1869

MCCARTHY LIVERY AND STABLES, BANE, NEVADA

Isaac tossed and turned the entire night. His mind ran through a multitude of scenarios, all of which resulted in him and Lucy leaving but ultimately being found by her father and husband. While he had her love, they had insufficient resources to pull from. If he was going to run away with her, they too would need a vast fortune to leverage, but how could he amass such an amount in a short period of time.

His thoughts kept drifting back to the mine and to silver. Then an idea came to him, but if he was going to pull it off, he'd need the one and only person he could trust, who was also the only person who knew who he truly was: Connor.

Isaac banged on the door until someone answered.

"What do ya want?" Duncan howled.

"I'm looking for Connor."

The door creaked open and there stood Duncan, rubbing his swollen eyes. "Do you know what time it is?" Duncan snorted.

"I know it's early, but I need to speak with your brother right now. It's an emergency," Isaac said.

Duncan squinted and asked, "You're his friend, the

sheriff, aren't ya?"

"Yes, I'm Sheriff Travis," Isaac replied, pulling open his overcoat so the man could see his badge.

"I suppose it's a good thing for my brother to have the sheriff as his friend versus the opposite, unless you're coming here to take him in for God knows what. You do know he's an ex-convict, don't ya?"

Before Isaac could answer, Connor bellowed from the loft of the barn. "Shut your piehole, Duncan. The sheriff there is my friend. I'm sure he's here for a social visit."

Isaac looked past Duncan and finally saw Connor climbing down a ladder. "Connor, I need to talk with you."

"It must be urgent if you've come at this hour. Couldn't it wait until the sun rose?" Connor said, walking towards him while scratching his butt.

"There's no time to waste," Isaac answered.

Connor slapped Duncan on the shoulder and said, "Invite the man in, ya damn fool, and go make us a pot of tea. Make yourself useful."

"I'm going back to bed. To hell with you two," Duncan said, walking off.

"Get inside. It's colder than a witch's tit out there," Connor said, a blanket draped over his shoulders.

Isaac stepped inside and closed the large door behind him.

"Come with me to the back. We can sit down," Connor said then grabbed a lantern from near the door to guide the way.

"It's good to see you," Isaac said.

The two sat down on straw bales in the back.

"What can I do for ya, Sheriff?" Connor asked.

"I need you."

"You know how to make a man feel special, don't ya?" Connor laughed.

"She loves me," Isaac declared.

Connor stood up immediately and said, "Show yourself out. I'm not here to listen to more mushy boy-like talk."

"Fine, how would you like to potentially make a lot of money?" Isaac asked.

"Now you're talking my language," Connor said, sitting back down.

"It's possibly dangerous," Isaac said.

"Dangerous? That sounds exciting after working two days or so in a barn with horses. Risking my life sounds like an adventure."

"It would require you to work for me as a deputy," Isaac said.

"A deputy? Does it pay well?" Connor asked.

Isaac cocked his head in disbelief. "Did you not hear what I said about making a lot of money?"

"Yes, right, correct. Go ahead. And yes, I want to make a lot of money."

"There's only potential, but you will be compensated fairly if it doesn't work out," Isaac said.

"Count me in," Connor said.

"What about your brother?" Isaac asked.

From the loft, Duncan hollered, "Take him with ya.

He's been worthless here."

"Oh, to hell with ya," Connor spat.

"It's only temporary, so he'll be returning, Duncan," Isaac said.

"Keep him as long as you want," Duncan replied.

"My family is so loving." Connor laughed. "So tell me, what am I to be doing?"

"It concerns a silver shipment that was stolen. We're going to try to find it," Isaac said.

"And if we find it, do we keep it?" Connor asked.

"Exactly," Isaac said.

SHERIFF'S OFFICE, BANE, NEVADA

Filled with a strong sense of purpose, Isaac went to work ready to put together the remaining part of his plan. With time limited, he had none to waste.

As he was dismounting, he spotted an unlikely pair: Marcus and Edwin. The two were huddled close outside Smith's Mercantile. Finding it odd, he watched them. Edwin appeared frantic, his hands and mouth moving wildly, while Marcus stood tall and motionless as usual.

He cinched his horse to the post and kept watching. What could they be discussing? he wondered. They were both the top lieutenants for two men who despised each other. Were they working on some sort of truce? Were they concocting a scheme behind their illustrious leaders' backs? And could he use it to his advantage? He made a point to find out, and the one person he knew would open up was Edwin.

"Morning, Sheriff," Wallace said as he exited the sheriff's office.

"Deputy, how are you today?" Isaac asked.

"All's well. I have a fella in here says he's your friend. He's got a weird accent," Wallace said.

"His name is Connor and he's a new deputy. How are we doing getting the remaining deputies?" Isaac asked. He glanced quickly over to Marcus and Edwin and saw they were now gone.

"We'll have everyone by the end of the day."

"How many do we have now?"

"Eighteen," Wallace replied.

"Are they all here?" Isaac asked.

"All but a couple who worked last night," Wallace answered.

Isaac hopped onto the walkway, pushed by Wallace, and entered the office. Gathered all around was the gaggle of new hires. By the looks of them, they were all former miners.

"I've given them all a talking to. They know what we expect out of them," Wallace said.

"Firearms? Do we have enough firearms for them all?" Isaac asked.

"No," Wallace answered.

"Go to Smith's Merc and buy all he has, and if that's not enough, go find more. We need these men armed," Isaac ordered.

"Yes, Sheriff," Wallace said, departing the office.

"Show of hands how many fought during the war?" Isaac asked.

Two-thirds of the men raised their hands.

"This son of a bitch here is a rebel, thought ya should know, Sheriff," a man bellowed, his index finger pointed at a man near the corner of the room.

"I don't give a damn. We're all Americans now, and if you didn't know, I was a Confederate too," Isaac said, keeping his role-playing in mind.

The man closed his mouth and looked down sheepishly.

"Now line up. I want to chat with each of you; then I'll assign you to the tasks I have in mind," Isaac said, taking a seat at his desk.

One by one, Isaac interviewed each man. He made copious notes, and when he was finished, he made a list of where each would work. Those men who claimed to be veterans, he narrowed down further. He needed a team of men whom he thought capable who would ride with Connor.

Wallace appeared holding a crate. "I cleaned Smith out. Got nine Army Colts and four Navys."

"Good, now look at this list and assign a firearm to each of the men who has a check mark," Isaac ordered.

"Whatcha have in mind, Sheriff?" Wallace asked.

"We're taking back this town one deputy at a time. And in order to do that, we need to have a sizable force. Now I'm putting you in charge of providing law enforcement for the town, Connor will take charge of the roads in, and I'll begin focusing on who stole the silver shipment so we can find it."

"But, Sheriff, that shipment is long gone. You'll

never find it now," Wallace said.

Isaac patted his shoulder and said, "I don't like the word *never*, so let's refrain from using it."

"Yes, Sheriff."

"You all have your responsibilities; now get to it," Isaac barked to his deputies.

Everyone began to hustle, a sense of pride in them all.

A smile creased Isaac's face. He was enjoying his role as a sheriff; he never imagined he'd be in this position and felt he was adapting to it quite well.

CORRIGAN MINING COMPANY OFFICE, BANE, NEVADA

A crisp chill swept across Mortimer's face as he walked to his office, reminding him that soon snow would start to fall, greatly slowing the entire operation. With the smelter down, he'd be even further behind. Although he could sell the raw ore, it garnered him greater profit to melt it down and extract the pure silver.

Having his new sheriff provided him much relief; his sleepless nights were now gone. It wasn't that he was stress-free, he just had a few less things to focus on, giving him time to manage the reconstruction of the smelting facility and prepare the presentation he'd give to Everett upon his arrival.

Mortimer entered his office to find Edwin sitting in a chair in front of his desk. He appeared anxious as he chewed on his fingernails. "Is everything okay?"

Unable to look at Mortimer, Edwin answered, "Fine, everything is fine."

Mortimer hung up his overcoat and took a seat behind his desk. "Ed, you don't look fine. What ails you?"

"Nothing, I'm fine," Edwin snapped.

Not used to seeing Edwin act this way, Mortimer pried. "You can always talk to me. You know that?"

"I've been looking into that parcel of land Mr. Wilkes is buying, and it appears it's worthless. I don't suggest you purchase it."

"What's wrong with it?" Mortimer asked.

"The men I sent out came back and said it's worthless," Edwin said.

"Worthless? Seems odd that Wilkes would move to purchase something without his own due diligence," Mortimer said. He got up and began to pace. "Let's send out another team; get them over there. I need to know about this parcel. If it truly has value, I want to buy it out from underneath Wilkes."

"But my men said—"

"I heard you, Edwin, just send another team and do it fast," Mortimer said.

"Yes, sir."

"Seriously, what is wrong with you today? You look like you're not sleeping," Mortimer asked.

"I haven't been feeling well; I'm sure that's it," Edwin replied.

"Go see the doc today after you've gotten everything else done," Mortimer said.

Getting to his feet, Edwin said, "I'll do that."

Giving Edwin a glance, Mortimer asked, "You'd tell me if something was wrong, wouldn't you?"

"I would, sir."

"Good, now go get those men out to that land. I want to know by tomorrow night at the latest," Mortimer said.

Stopping at the door, Edwin said, "You'll know by tomorrow."

CORRIGAN RESIDENCE, BANE, NEVADA

Isaac entered the house. His nostrils flared when the savory aroma from the kitchen wafted over him. His mouth watered and his stomach churned.

"Sheriff Travis, good to see you," Phyllis said, walking around and taking his coat. "Supper will be on the table in fifteen minutes. Mrs. Corrigan was concerned you may not make it tonight."

Isaac smoothed his hair with his hand and adjusted his gun belt. "I'm here now."

Looking down at his holstered pistol, Phyllis said, "Best you go get cleaned up and put that away. I don't think Mrs. Corrigan wants firearms at her dinner table."

Isaac glanced down and said, "You're right. I'll go get washed and more presentable."

"Sheriff, is that you?" Mortimer called out from the parlor.

"I suppose I'll do that after I speak with him," Isaac said, smiling to Phyllis. He entered the parlor to find Mortimer seated in his favorite wing-back chair, a pipe in his hand. "Grab a drink and join me."

"Can I do that after I get cleaned up?" Isaac asked.

"No, get in here and give me an update," Mortimer said.

Feeling he had no choice, Isaac poured a glass of whiskey and sat down in the opposite chair. "When I left the office, we had finished hiring our last people. I spent the greater part of the day filling those special teams. No other word concerning Wilkes, and nothing about the silver either."

"The town seems to have settled down since your arrival. No shootings or stabbings, just your typical fisticuffs at the saloons," Mortimer said.

"Did I mention I'm having each supply train escorted through the pass?" Isaac asked.

"Yes, you did. That's a very good idea. Once those bandits get wind, we should see things settle down there as well," Mortimer said. "And did you send a team with a private coach to pick up Mr. Wagner?"

"I did," Isaac said. The reminder that he had little time made him tense.

"Good," Mortimer said.

Isaac took a large gulp and said, "I really should get cleaned up. I shouldn't show up at your table covered in dust."

Mortimer glanced at Isaac and said, "Go ahead. I'll see you in the dining room."

Isaac put his glass down and left the room. As he headed towards his room, he looked up and spotted Lucy watching him. He stopped and waved.

She waved back.

The two stared at each other until Phyllis came into the hallway holding a serving dish.

"Sheriff Travis, you best hurry. You only have five minutes," Phyllis said and disappeared into the dining room.

Isaac looked up, but this time Lucy was gone. He went to his room and got ready.

***

Dinner was filled with laughter and great conversation. It appeared to Isaac that Lucy was her old self in many ways. He'd say something and she'd follow up with something pithy and sarcastic. Even Mortimer was taking notice of her changed behavior.

"You're feeling better, I see," Mortimer said.

"I am," she said, leaning over and touching his hand.

Catching sight of that made Isaac recoil. He'd never seen her act affectionately towards Mortimer until that moment.

Mortimer followed by intertwining his fingers with hers.

This made Isaac feel even more repulsed. Why was she doing this in front of him? he thought.

"I can't express how good it feels to see you so chipper and, dare I say, happy," Mortimer said.

Leaning back in her chair, Lucy said, "I woke this morning and everything felt right. I had an epiphany of sorts, I suppose."

"You did?" Mortimer asked.

Looking deeply into his eyes, she said, "I love you, and I so want to tell you how sorry I am that I've been ill for these long months. It wasn't fair to you, my dear husband."

A nauseous feeling set in for Isaac. Was she trying to upset him? Confused by her actions, he stood up abruptly and said, "If you'll excuse me."

"Is everything alright? You look piqued," Mortimer said.

"Yes, are you well, Sheriff?" Lucy asked.

Isaac shot her a look and said, "I'm just feeling a bit under the weather suddenly."

"Hmm, shall I call a doctor?" Mortimer asked, concerned.

"I think I just need to get a good night's rest. I've been going really hard since I arrived," Isaac lied.

"Shall I have Phyllis draw you a hot bath?" Lucy asked, a crooked smile on her face.

"Mrs. Corrigan, that won't be necessary, but thank you nonetheless," Isaac said sharply.

Sensing something was off, Mortimer rose and said, "Come, let us walk. Maybe some fresh air will do you good."

Looking at him then her, Isaac said, "Yes, let's go for a walk."

Lucy hopped to her feet and said, "Husband, let the poor sheriff go rest. If he's getting ill, you don't want him walking in the chill of night."

"I suppose that's true," Mortimer said.

"It's fine, Mortimer. I'll go by myself," Isaac said. He went to the foyer, put on his coat, and headed out the front door.

Outside, the crisp night air was like a smack in the face. He walked down the front steps and stood looking towards the lights of town below. He tried to find an explanation for Lucy's behavior and could only surmise she meant what she said in the letter and that she really wanted him to go so badly that she'd make it uncomfortable for him to be around her.

But didn't she know her actions would bring him pain? Seeing her show another man affection was like stabbing him in the heart with a knife and twisting the blade. It was one thing to imagine, another to witness it occur. Then another theory came to mind. Was she merely deflecting? Was she showing Mortimer much-needed attention as a way to allow Isaac to implement his plan? But after more thought, that didn't make sense, as she wasn't aware of his plan.

Distraught, he sat on the bottom step and looked to the twinkling stars above. If she did desire him to go, then what was the point of staying? Should he find a horse and make for the coast? Filled with confusion, he allowed his thoughts to drift.

The minutes turned to hours before he suddenly came to a conclusion. If he was going to leave Bane without her, he'd come to that decision based upon the reality that she truly didn't want to be with him, not an emotional reaction to the events of the evening.

His plagued thoughts were torn to the present when

he heard footfalls in the darkness beyond. "Who goes there?"

"Sheriff, is that you?" Connor asked, suddenly and surprisingly emerging from the black of night.

"What are you doing here?" Isaac asked, shocked to see him of all people at the house.

"I was having a bit to drink down at the saloon, and I had an idea. I like to think it's a brilliant idea since it came from my head, and I couldn't wait to tell ya, so I headed up to see ya."

"You do know I'm staying here as a guest; this isn't my house. You can't come calling at any hour," Isaac said, getting up and walking over towards Connor to prevent him from getting any closer to the house.

"It's cold. Can we go inside?" Connor asked.

"I'm afraid not. Why don't you tell me what's on your mind?" Isaac asked.

Connor produced a bottle and put it to his mouth. He guzzled a fair amount then offered some to Isaac. "Care for a nip?"

"I'm fine. Just tell me what you're doing here," Isaac said, concerned about having someone as loud as Connor outside Mortimer's house.

"I was standing in the saloon and the thought came as to what we could do with that silver when we find it," Connor said, his speech slurred.

"Please keep your voice down. You do know that silver is his," Isaac said, pointing to the house behind him.

Connor lifted the bottle and said, "Well, how do you

do, Mr. Rich Man in the Big House."

"Damn it, Connor, keep your voice down," Isaac said, his tone chastising.

Leaning his weight on Isaac, Connor said, "So do you want to know my idea?"

"No, I don't. What I want you to do is go get some sleep. You were supposed to be getting your team ready to ride out late tomorrow, not getting drunk."

"My team is fine, a fine bunch of young men. I really want to thank you for giving me this opportunity," Connor said, his speech becoming more slurred.

Isaac swung his arm over Connor's shoulder and began to lead him down the drive.

"I don't think you want to discuss my idea," Connor said just as he slipped, bringing both men to the ground hard.

Aggravated with Connor, Isaac got to his feet and barked, "Damn it, Connor. I wouldn't have brought you on if I knew you were a drunk."

"I'm not a drunk, I just like to drink," Connor said. He was laid out on his back.

Isaac got him to his feet and said, "Go get some rest. We'll talk in the morning."

Pushing Isaac away, Connor said, "Fine, but you're missing out on a good idea. Maybe I'll get my daft brother Duncan on board with it. I can't imagine he wants to run a livery the rest of his life."

"Goodnight, Connor," Isaac said. He watched Connor disappear into the darkness.

Frustrated by Connor's unwelcome appearance at the

house, Isaac went back inside and prayed no one had heard. The house was now dark save for a couple of lanterns turned down to just a glow. He peeked his head inside the parlor, but it was empty. He made his way to his room. All he wanted to do was sleep so that he could wake up to a better day than this one had been.

CHAPTER EIGHT

NOVEMBER 1, 1869

TRIPLE B HOTEL, BANE, NEVADA

"It's not my fault. I had no idea he'd press me to have another team of men inspect that parcel," Edwin complained, his head in his hands.

Marcus sat across from him, his hands placed palm down on his lap. "It doesn't matter. By the end of the day we will be partners with those businessmen, not Wilkes or Corrigan," Marcus said, trying to reassure Edwin.

"Why are we doing this? Why do you want to keep the property now and not sell it to Mr. Corrigan?" Edwin asked, confused. "I don't want to own part of a mining company."

The two had partnered up some weeks ago after Edwin had approached a delusional Marcus in the saloon. Though Edwin seemed content, he was far from it. He perceived Mortimer as unworthy and thought if a man like him could be rich, so could he. Marcus expressed his dissatisfaction with Wilkes, and they set forth to make an unusual partnership. Marcus divulged the land and mining-company deal Quincy was working on. This set in motion the plan to acquire the land out from underneath Quincy then sell it at a premium to Mortimer without either knowing who had purchased it. They'd finance the land deal with the silver they had stolen from Quincy. Neither expressed a desire to be a part of this proposed silver-mining operation—that was until yesterday when Marcus told Edwin the plan had changed and he wished to open the operation with the businessmen.

"I want to do it, that's all. If you want, I'll buy you out of your share when I make my first sale of silver," Marcus said.

"I don't want to own a silver mine. I want the money so I can leave this Godforsaken place," Edwin exclaimed.

"You can leave. I'll buy you out for a cheaper price; then you can be on your merry way," Marcus said.

"No, I'm not getting ripped off here. I've risked everything. I just don't like when well-thought-out plans are changed at the last minute," Edwin barked.

"I know you're upset, but you need to move past this," Marcus said calmly.

"I didn't want the general public to know I'm the owner, but now it will happen. This wasn't the plan, this wasn't the plan!" Edwin cried out.

"Plans change. I've given you your options; take it or leave it," Marcus said soberly.

Frustrated, Edwin hopped to his feet and paced the small hotel room. "This was supposed to be easy."

"Easy for you. Securing the silver took hard work," Marcus said.

"Don't give me talk about hard work. You didn't steal it back; it was men we hired," Edwin said.

"I set it all up, not you," Marcus said.

"And I almost set up Mortimer to buy it from us

until you decided you wanted to go into business with men we don't know, running a company we have no idea how to run," Edwin groveled.

"We can be rich, filthy rich. There's silver in that mountain, and we'll be the ones who own it," Marcus said, his thoughts of wealth exciting him.

"First of all, it won't just be yours or ours, we're going into business with those men, and that makes the shares split six ways. And second, you don't care about the potential windfall. What you want to do is flaunt this in front of Wilkes, but you don't know what he'll do; he's powerful," Edwin said.

"He's only powerful because I've shielded him with a small army of men that I hired, I built—me, not him. Those men are loyal to me," Marcus said.

"Those men are loyal to money, don't fool yourself," Edwin complained.

"Maybe so, but we have the money to hire them and make them ours. Before I step into that meeting later today, I'll have my own army of men to protect us," Marcus said.

Edwin stopped and thought. "Where's the silver?"

"Somewhere safe," Marcus replied.

"Tell me, I deserve to know," Edwin insisted.

"You don't need to concern yourself with that," Marcus said.

"It's here, isn't it? In town somewhere," Edwin said.

"Yes."

"Where?" Edwin asked.

"Like I said, somewhere safe," Marcus replied.

Edwin thought for a moment then fired back, "It's at the stables. You've hidden it underneath Wilkes' nose at the stables that Scotsman is leasing from Wilkes."

Marcus gritted his teeth.

"For someone who normally has a poker face, you just gave me a tell. It's at the livery somewhere," Edwin proclaimed.

"Don't you dare say a damn word," Marcus cursed, which was unlike him.

"Unfortunately, Marcus, I'm too involved to tell anyone. I'm in this with you all the way. But damn it, we had a plan, and you had to spoil it because you just had to rub it in his face. The plan was coming together, use some of the money, buy the parcel of land from the owner in California, split the remaining silver, then sell the parcel to Mortimer for a premium and split that; we'd both be rich and go our own ways. Now I'm tied to this, to you, to this damn area."

"How many times do I have to say that plans change? And you have an out; take it or shut up."

"How do I know you won't double-cross me?"

"The same way I don't know if you will," Marcus answered and stood. "This conversation is boring. Can you please leave?"

Edwin removed his pocket watch and checked the time. "Is the meeting still set for ten o'clock this morning, or has that changed too?" Edwin scoffed.

"It's still ten."

"I'll be there, and please don't make any other changes to the plan," Edwin said before leaving.

Marcus stared at the door. He didn't trust Edwin, and now that Edwin knew exactly where the silver was hidden, Marcus needed to ensure that it didn't disappear. He grabbed his hat and headed out.

BANE, NEVADA

Hoping to run into Lucy on his way out of the house, Isaac deliberately made more noise than normal. However, all he accomplished was stirring Phyllis, who emerged from the kitchen with twenty questions.

After escaping Phyllis' endless doting and chatter, he made for the office, his mind plagued by how to proceed. Normally, when he encountered uncertainty, Isaac just went with the strategy in place until something more definitive made itself known; so he found no reason yet to change.

His ride to the office was a chilly one. The air was dry and cool, far different than what he was used to in New York. As he trotted up to the office, he spotted Edwin leaving the Triple B Hotel and instantly recalled seeing him engaged in a heated conversation with Marcus. If he couldn't keep pushing his plan, he'd at least keep pretending to be sheriff and do what Mortimer had hired Travis for.

"Edwin, hold up!" Isaac hollered.

Edwin stopped and gave Isaac a frightened stare.

"Come over here. I want to chat with you," Isaac said before dismounting.

"I'm busy, sorry," Edwin said as he kept his pace

brisk.

"Edwin, come here…now!" Isaac demanded. He had a sense that something was off about Edwin.

Keeping his distance, Edwin replied, "Can this wait, Sheriff?"

"No, it can't. Meet me in the office, now," Isaac said, tying his horse to the post.

Edwin sighed then sauntered over. "Sheriff, I'm very busy. I'm doing something urgent for Mr. Corrigan."

"Edwin, I can assure you that anything I do, including pulling you aside, will get Mr. Corrigan's blessing. Now please step inside the office."

Sheepishly, Edwin agreed and headed inside.

Wallace jumped up from behind a desk and said, "Morning, Sheriff and Edwin."

"Good morning, Deputy, can you get me and Edwin a hot cup of coffee?" Isaac asked.

"Sure thing, there's some on the stove here," Wallace said, racing off to get it.

"Take a seat," Isaac said, motioning to a small armless wooden chair in front of his oak desk.

Sitting down, Edwin twirled his hat and kept his gaze towards the floor.

Isaac removed his hat and coat and took a seat at his desk. "Edwin, how are you doing?"

"I'm fine, Sheriff."

Wallace brought over two steaming cups of coffee and set them on the desk. "Anything else, Sheriff?"

"Give us privacy," Isaac said.

Edwin's face became ashen when Isaac told Wallace

to leave.

Picking up on Edwin's peculiar behavior, Isaac pressed the question he wanted a clear answer on. "I saw you talking with Wilkes' man Marcus. The conversation looked heated. Why were you talking to him?"

Edwin gulped and said, "We, ah, we were discussing plans about…" Edwin paused, unable to think of a good lie that would make sense. "We, um, I needed to run something by him concerning a parcel of land Mortimer wishes to purchase."

"Is that true?" Isaac asked.

"Yes, it's the truth. He's been providing me information about a land deal that Wilkes is working on."

"Does Mortimer know about this?"

"He does; however, he doesn't know whom I've been talking to," Edwin confessed.

"You realize that it looks very suspicious from my vantage point. You know why I was brought in here, and I need to follow up on anything that could help flush out who might have stolen the silver and burned down the barn," Isaac said.

"I understand, but could you do me a favor and not tell Mr. Corrigan?" Edwin asked.

"Why would I do that?" Isaac asked.

"Marcus is only working with me on the condition that it's anonymous," Edwin answered. "If he knows I've told you and Mr. Corrigan, it could jeopardize him and our plan."

"Our plan?"

"I'm referring to what Mr. Corrigan is trying to do,"

Edwin replied.

"And that is?" Isaac asked.

"To buy the land from underneath Wilkes," Edwin said honestly.

Isaac leaned back in his chair and stared hard at Edwin. He spotted a bead of sweat on his brow and asked, "You seem nervous?"

"Because I'm being interrogated."

"I'm not interrogating you, I'm merely asking some questions," Isaac said.

Growing agitated, Edwin stood, his fingers clinging to his hat. "If you're done, I'd like to get back to what I was doing."

"Who were you visiting at the Triple B?" Isaac asked.

"So now my personal business is also to be known?" Edwin asked defensively.

"Were you visiting a prostitute?" Isaac asked.

Edwin's face flushed. "Sir, I'm through with this undignified line of questions." He turned and made for the door.

"Edwin, I didn't say you could leave," Isaac pressed.

"I don't work for you, I work for Mr. Corrigan," Edwin blared.

"So do I, and I intend on going to him right away and telling him my concerns about your trustworthiness."

"Sheriff Travis, I expressed my reluctance about hiring you. Your reputation is, as they say, that you're brash, rude and…"

"And? Please keep insulting me," Isaac joked.

"You're indignant!"

"Your response to simple questions is very telling," Isaac said, sensing that Edwin was hiding something crucial.

"Good day, Sheriff," Edwin snapped. He threw open the door and angrily exited, slamming the door behind him.

Isaac intertwined his fingers and pondered the exchange. His instinct that Edwin was up to no good was all but confirmed by his conduct. Needing to know where he went from there, he hopped up and exited the office to find Wallace sitting outside, his feet propped up against a pillar. "Deputy, I need you to man the office."

"Okay, Sheriff, where are you off to?" Wallace asked.

"I'm going to see what our friend Edwin does today," Isaac said.

"You're going to follow him?" Wallace asked, intrigued by the idea. "Is something going on?"

"There might be some trouble brewing. Keep your head on straight today," Isaac said.

Tipping his hat, Wallace said, "I'll hold the fort down."

Connor's team came around the corner and approached the office.

"Good morning, Sheriff, is Connor here yet?" one of the men asked.

"No, he's not," Isaac said.

"He's an hour late. He told us yesterday to be here then, and he hasn't shown up. We waited then decided to go get some breakfast at the hotel," the man said.

"I'll find out where he is while I'm out. Head inside

and wait." Isaac sighed then headed off to follow Edwin.

MCCARTHY LIVERY AND STABLES, BANE, NEVADA

Marcus entered the darkened and musty stables. He looked around but saw no one. "Anyone here?"

Popping his head around the corner near the back, Duncan replied, "What can I do for ya?"

"I need to get that wagon I dropped off the other day," Marcus said to Duncan.

"Yes, the wagon. I'll pull it around," Duncan offered.

"Not necessary. I'll bring my horse over and move it out myself," Marcus said.

"If that works for ya, sure," Duncan said. "Follow me."

The two walked through the stables, out the back and to the smaller barn adjacent. Duncan unlocked the large brass lock and removed a chain that held the two large doors together. He opened them, allowing the early morning light to illuminate the wagon and other stored items inside.

"You need any help at all?" Duncan asked.

"I'll be fine. What do I owe you?" Marcus asked.

"Five dollars will do it," Duncan said.

Marcus pulled a few coins from his pocket and handed them to Duncan. "Keep the change."

"Why, thank you, pleasure doing business with you. Do store your wares anytime you need to," Duncan said with a broad smile.

Marcus nodded and went to work cinching up his horse to the wagon.

Duncan returned to the stables to find Edwin standing there. "Hello, fine sir, how can I help you?"

"There was a wagon stored here the other day; I'm here to retrieve it for my friend Marcus Burner," Edwin said, clearly intent on stealing the silver out from underneath Marcus.

Duncan furrowed his brow and gave Edwin a puzzled look. "That's odd. He's…"

"He's here now, isn't he?" Edwin said.

Duncan pointed behind him and said, "Yes, he's pulling the wagon out as we speak."

"Liar and thief," Edwin said, pushing past Duncan. He ran through the stables and out the back. There he encountered Marcus climbing onto the wagon. "You were going to steal it for yourself!"

"You're wrong. I was merely removing the temptation from you," Marcus replied. "And might I ask what you're doing here?"

"I was…I was here to check on it, make sure it was safe," Edwin lied.

"I think you're the liar and thief. You came here to steal it," Marcus said.

Edwin reached inside his coat and pulled out a Colt 1862 Pocket Navy. It was a familiar .36-caliber round ball revolver with a short barrel. He cocked it and pointed it at Marcus. "Get off the wagon!"

"You're making a big mistake," Marcus said calmly, raising his hands slowly.

"Off the wagon, now!" Edwin yelled.

Duncan appeared and yelped in surprise upon seeing Edwin holding a gun on Marcus. "Easy, son, easy."

Edwin looked over his shoulder and hollered, "Get out of here!"

With Edwin distracted, Marcus ripped his Colt Dragoon from his holster, cocked it, took aim and fired.

The .44-caliber round ball exploded from the barrel and struck Edwin in the right shoulder. The impact was enough for Edwin to drop his pistol, which he'd been holding in his right hand. He bent over in pain and cried out.

Marcus cocked the Dragoon again, aimed and said, "I warned you." He squeezed the trigger again. This time the round struck Edwin in the neck; it traveled through his throat, exiting the opposite side. A large splatter of blood hit the barn door.

Edwin clutched his throat and gagged. Blood poured from his mouth. He dropped to his knees and gagged a bit more before falling face-first onto the hard dirt, dead.

"You killed the lad," Duncan cried out.

Marcus cocked his pistol one more time, aimed at Duncan, and said, "And I'll kill you if you utter a word."

"You won't get a word out of me, I swear on the Virgin Mary," Duncan said.

Connor emerged from the stables, rubbing his eyes. He saw Edwin on the ground surrounded by a pool of blood. He glanced up and saw Marcus aiming his pistol at Duncan. "No need to shoot anyone else."

"Just get out of my way and let me get on my way,"

Marcus ordered, switching his aim between Duncan and Connor.

"You'll have no trouble out of us," Connor said.

Marcus picked up the reins with his left hand, keeping his pistol extended out in front of him and trained on the brothers.

The click of a hammer being drawn back sounded in the alleyway.

Marcus quickly looked and saw Isaac standing with his Remington pointed directly at him.

"But you'll get trouble from me," Isaac said, his right eye aiming over the barrel and at Marcus' chest.

"Now, Sheriff, I shot him in self-defense. You ask the stable owner; he saw it all," Marcus said, his pistol still directed at the brothers.

"Put down your pistol and we can discuss this," Isaac said.

"I just want to move my wagon out of here, and later I can come visit you concerning this incident," Marcus said.

"I'm afraid that's not going to happen. Put down the pistol and hop off the wagon. Do it. Do it now," Isaac ordered.

"C'mon, Sheriff, this was in self-defense," Marcus pleaded. "Let me be on my way. I have business out of town and I'm running late."

"You'll just have to be a bit later," Isaac said.

Marcus exhaled heavily. He slowly lowered his arm then abruptly pivoted on the bench seat of the wagon and swung the barrel towards Isaac.

The move was a foolish one. Isaac simply squeezed the trigger and fired the .44-caliber pistol. His aim was true and the round struck Marcus squarely in the chest.

Marcus coughed a few times; then blood drooled from his open mouth. "You shot..." he mumbled before dropping his pistol onto the ground. He toppled over and off the wagon, landing on his head and shoulder.

Isaac cocked his pistol again and advanced. When he reached Marcus, he was dead.

"Well, isn't that a wake-up call!" Connor howled in joy as if he'd just experienced a thrilling show.

Duncan stood in shock. He'd heard about shootings in town, but this was the first time he'd witnessed a man being killed.

Isaac uncocked his pistol and holstered it. He bent down to confirm Marcus was dead by searching for a pulse on his neck.

Connor walked over and stood above the body. "You killed him, Sheriff."

Looking up, Isaac said, "I sure did."

"What the hell was so important in this wagon?" Connor asked, walking over and looking inside the covered wagon.

"Did you see the other shooting?" Isaac asked Duncan.

"I did. This man here had a gun on Marcus, and I distracted that man, giving Marcus time to draw and shoot him," Duncan explained.

"Oh, Sheriff, you need to come see this," Connor said.

Isaac walked around to the back of the wagon. He peeked inside to find Connor standing above several open trunks filled with silver bars. "Is that?"

"I think it's the silver we were looking for," Connor said.

"It sure is," Isaac said, pointing at the stenciled name on the side of a trunk.

"Corrigan Mining Company. Yep, this is the silver," Connor howled happily. "Praise be all the saints and the baby Jesus."

Duncan appeared and said, "We best tell Mr. Corrigan."

"No, no, that's not what we're doing, big brother," Connor said, jumping over the trunks until he reached Duncan. "This here silver is now ours."

"Sheriff, we can't keep this," Duncan said, looking to Isaac to back him up.

"Your brother is right. We're not turning this over...just yet. Not until I can confirm it's his," Isaac said, deliberately being misleading.

"You said if we found it, we'd keep it. You said I could make a lot of money, and this is the money," Connor argued.

"The silver isn't ours, it's Mr. Corrigan's," Duncan barked. "If they find out we kept it, we'll hang."

"They won't find out because no one knows we have it except you, me and the sheriff," Connor said.

"I'll tell him myself," Duncan said.

Pulling Duncan aside, Isaac explained, "Let me first confirm this is his, and if it is, we'll return it; if it's not, we might keep it."

"But that's not what you said," Connor said, openly challenging Isaac.

"It's someone's and most certainly stolen," Duncan said.

"Stop being straight as an arrow. This silver will set us up for life," Connor barked at his brother.

"And it could end our lives," Duncan shot back.

"Stop, enough. We will keep the silver hidden in the barn like it is. I'll confirm if it's Mr. Corrigan's, and if it is, we'll return it to him. What I don't need you doing, Duncan, is talking to anyone. This silver is now part of an investigation, and I don't need you spreading rumors and disrupting what I'm doing. Do you understand?"

Giving Isaac a leery look, Duncan replied, "I won't say a word, Sheriff, but we're not keeping this in my barn. Take it with you and hide it somewhere else. I don't want to be involved with this; just keep me out of it."

"I'll honor that," Isaac said.

"We don't want you around anyway," Connor said, closing the trunks and jumping out of the back of the wagon.

"What do I do about the bodies?" Duncan asked.

"Connor will take care of them, won't you, partner?" Isaac said, climbing onto the wagon.

Placing his hands on his hips and grunting, Connor replied, "I'll need compensation for doing it."

Raising his hands as if surrendering, Duncan said, "I don't want to know anything. Don't tell me a thing." He walked off, disappearing inside the stables.

"Where are you going to stash the wagon?" Connor asked.

"Not sure, do you have any ideas?" Isaac asked.

"I don't, and where am I supposed to dump them?" Connor asked, pointing to the bodies.

"I don't know," Isaac replied. He was now feeling a bit out of his element. By not reporting the recovered silver and the bodies, he wasn't only violating his oath and most certainly some law; but he was going against the mandate Mortimer had given him. He was acting like a criminal, the very thing he said he wasn't. Stewing on it for more than a few minutes, he said, "Toss the bodies in the back of the wagon."

"What are you going to do with them?" Connor asked.

He sighed loudly and said, "I'm turning everything in, I have to."

"What?"

"I'll compensate you for your troubles," Isaac said, feeling better that he was doing what was right.

Agitated, Connor blared, "If you're turning that silver over to Corrigan, you can load up the bodies yourself."

"Help me, Connor, I'll pay you," Isaac said, feeling bad that he was going against the plan he'd set up with Connor.

"I'm done being a deputy for you…Sheriff," Connor said, strutting off.

Isaac loaded the bodies into the back of the wagon and headed for Mortimer's office in town.

CORRIGAN MINING COMPANY OFFICE, BANE, NEVADA

During the short ride, Isaac batted around the idea of keeping the silver, but each time he convinced himself to do so, his conscience would scream in his head to do the right thing.

He parked the wagon in front of Mortimer's office and hopped off. Again he paused and thought about what he was about to do. By turning the silver over, he'd give up the one chance for him and Lucy to run off. Without the vast fortune that sat in the back of the wagon, he'd be unable to provide for her or compete with Mortimer and Everett.

From inside, Mortimer saw Isaac and waved.

Isaac simply nodded.

Again Mortimer waved, this time motioning for Isaac to come inside.

Knowing he couldn't stand outside, Isaac made up his mind and headed inside the offices.

Meeting him at the door, Mortimer said, "Good day, Sheriff."

"Can we speak in private in your office?" Isaac asked.

"Yes, please come in and take a seat," Mortimer said.

Isaac walked into the office with Mortimer just behind him, closing the door after himself. "If this is about last night, I don't think you have to apologize. You didn't feel well, and those odd afflictions can affect us all."

"I found the silver," Isaac blurted out.

Mortimer's mouth jutted open in shock at the unexpected news. "You found the silver, my silver?"

"Yes."

"Where was it? Who had it?"

"And you should know now that Edwin is dead, murdered," Isaac said, revealing all the news up front with no filter.

"Dead? How? Are the two related?" Mortimer asked.

"Yes."

"Sheriff, you're being a man of few words. I know you Texans pride yourself on that sort of thing, but I need details. Tell me everything, and please, please tell me that Wilkes was involved in this."

"I believe he might be," Isaac said, answering as honestly as he could, but based upon his own experience in being wrongfully accused, he went further. "However, I don't know for sure."

"Tell me everything. I need to know, tell me," Mortimer said, leaning across his desk.

Isaac hadn't thought about how he'd address the Edwin situation and his suspicions concerning him. Should he mislead, or should he divulge all he knew and suspected?

"Well?" Mortimer asked, his hands clasped tight in anticipation. Something caught his eye and he looked outside again. He put his focus on the wagon and continued, "Is my silver in that wagon?" He stood up and headed for the door.

Isaac got up and followed him.

The two went outside, with Mortimer tossing the canvas flap aside to look inside. "That's my silver, and that's Edwin and Marcus." His eyes fixed on Edwin's eyes, which lay open in a deathly stare.

"I found it at the livery. The wagon was being stored there," Isaac said.

"Have you arrested that filthy Scot for being an accomplice?" Mortimer asked.

"No."

Giving Isaac an odd look, Mortimer asked, "Why not? He's surely involved."

"He's not. I know that for sure," Isaac said.

"Sheriff, I need you to be sure. I need everyone who was involved with this arrested, charged and, if found guilty, hanged."

"I will do everything in my power, but I can assure you that the McCarthy brothers had nothing to do with this," Isaac said.

"And no hard evidence to link Wilkes?" Mortimer asked.

"Only circumstantial," Isaac replied.

Ogling his silver once more, Mortimer said, "Tell me everything."

Isaac told him all he knew, the facts, his suspicions, and the exchange between Edwin and Marcus.

Confused, Mortimer asked, "And you're sure you heard him say it like that?"

"Yes, he said he was making sure it was safe," Isaac answered, his recollection crystal clear. He'd overheard their conversation as he walked up on the encounter, listening intently as the two exchanged comments.

"I can't believe Edwin helped steal my silver. He had information on the shipment, so that makes sense. He would have known how many men we were sending and the route once they were out of the mountain pass. And if he was working with Marcus, that has to mean Wilkes is a party to this," Mortimer declared.

"We don't know that for sure," Isaac said.

"Marcus is his right-hand man," Mortimer blared.

"And Edwin was yours. There could be an argument made you were a party to this," Isaac shot back, his senses telling him that the two men were operating alone.

"You're wrong, and the implication, even though used to illustrate a point, is insulting. Go arrest Wilkes and charge him with the theft of the silver and the murder of those deputies," Mortimer ordered.

"That would be premature," Isaac said.

"You work for me. Go and arrest him now! I want to see him behind bars within the hour!" Mortimer barked.

"But, Mortimer, I don't have anything linking him directly," Isaac countered. Falsely arresting anyone, even someone as notorious and low-down as Wilkes, for a crime he didn't commit didn't sit well with him.

"Arrest him now or I'll get someone who will," Mortimer shouted, his nostrils flared in anger.

Seeing Mortimer display this hate and vitriol was counter to the calm man he'd known the past few days.

After waiting for Isaac to respond, Mortimer snapped, "Well, Sheriff, are you going to do as I demand, or do I need to get Deputy Wallace to do it?"

Isaac thought about it and couldn't get himself to go against his gut instinct that the two men were working together; that didn't mean Wilkes was an innocent man, just that the altercation between Edwin and Marcus was separate from him.

"Sheriff, you're fired," Mortimer said, holding his hand out.

"You're letting me go? I just found your silver."

"Hand it over," Mortimer said, his hand still extended, palm up.

"What?"

"Your badge, I'm going to pin it on a man who I can trust to handle this situation accordingly," Mortimer said.

Defiant, Isaac said, "If you feel this strongly and wish to arrest a man without hard evidence, I can't be a part of that."

"That's fine. I've been needing something, something that I could link to Wilkes to finally take him down, and this is it," Mortimer said.

Isaac opened his overcoat, pulled the badge off, and placed it in Mortimer's hand. He looked at the glimmering badge and instantly missed having it grace his chest. He'd been sheriff for only a matter of days, yet he longed for the title. It was a strange feeling, one he couldn't place his finger on.

"I'll have Phyllis gather your belongings and have them at the doorstep for you to recover. Come by later and get your compensation, including the bonus I promised for finding my silver. I at least owe you that," Mortimer said.

Isaac stood speechless.

"Goodbye, Sheriff Travis," Mortimer said, turning around and strutting back inside his office.

Standing alone in the street, Isaac felt as if he were having an out-of-body experience. He could imagine himself floating above and glancing down at himself.

Seconds later a young man burst from Mortimer's office and sprinted down the street in the direction of the sheriff's office.

A feeling of defeat suddenly overwhelmed Isaac. He was closer than he had been to possibly winning over Lucy, only to surrender it because his integrity demanded it. Where was this integrity when he assumed Travis' identity? Where was it when he continuously lied to everyone he met in town? Now angry with himself for tossing aside a chance to win Lucy over, he headed back to the one place he could clear his thoughts, the Rusty Nail Saloon.

WILKES' OFFICE, BANE, NEVADA

Staring out across the long oak table at the four businessmen assembled, Quincy felt a surge of energy. He was as close as he'd ever been to being truly wealthy. It had taken him a lifetime to get here, and soon, he'd be like his nemesis Mortimer and those other rich barons back east.

"Gentlemen, thank you for coming all the way from San Francisco and beyond. As I've explained in numerous letters, we have a real opportunity to own and operate a silver mine that could produce for us millions of dollars in ore."

Commotion sounded in the front outside the boardroom.

All eyes turned to the door, waiting for it to explode open, by the sounds coming from the other side.

"Is a shoot-out about to commence in the other room?" one of the men joked.

Laughter broke out around the table, except from Quincy, who was growing more concerned the louder it became.

"If you'll excuse me, I need to see what's going on," Quincy said and headed for the door.

Before he could reach it, the door burst open, and in came Wallace sporting the sheriff's badge, followed by several deputies.

"What's this?" Quincy asked angrily.

"Quincy Wilkes, you're under arrest," Wallace announced.

Gasps came from the businessmen followed by whispers and crosstalk.

"This is absurd! For what?" Quincy howled in protest.

"For stealing the silver shipment and the murder of half a dozen deputies," Wallace answered.

Behind Wallace, the deputies who came with him had their pistols drawn.

"This is outrageous. I'm having a meeting with some very important people, and these ridiculous charges, no doubt brought by Mortimer Corrigan, will be challenged,"

Quincy cried out.

"Come with me," Wallace said, stepping towards Quincy.

Quincy stepped back and put his hands out in front of him. "Marcus, get in here. Help me."

"Marcus can't help you. He's dead," Wallace said.

"What? That's impossible," Quincy said, his anger turning to fear as he began to sense he'd been either double-crossed or they'd found something linking him to it all.

"Don't make this difficult, Mr. Wilkes," Wallace said, following Quincy as he kept backpedaling around the long table.

"I won't go. No, this was supposed to be my big day, no," Quincy whined as the fear now turned to anguish.

"Please, Mr. Wilkes, don't make this hard. I just want to take you in," Wallace said. He pointed to one of the deputies to go the other way so they could corner Quincy.

"Where's the sheriff? Why are you here and not him?" Quincy asked, noticing Wallace was wearing the badge.

"I'm the sheriff now," Wallace said.

"What's going on here? I've been set up. I've done nothing wrong. Gentlemen, please don't leave. I'll straighten this out in a short while, and we can continue afterwards," Quincy begged the men before him.

One of the businessmen, a man named Hannibal Guster, asked, "Where can we find this Mr. Corrigan?"

Pausing his advance, Wallace answered, "In his office in town."

"What office?"

"The Corrigan Mining Company office. He's the man who owns this town," Wallace said.

"Wait, no, don't go see him, no!" Quincy yelled, his back now up against the corner of the room.

Hannibal looked at the other men and said, "Let's not waste the trip here. Shall we go visit Mr. Corrigan?"

The other men nodded in agreement.

"No!" Quincy screamed, his veins popping in his neck and forehead.

Wallace and his deputy Ned grabbed Quincy, each taking an arm. They forcibly turned him around, shackled his wrists, and dragged him from the boardroom.

As he was being hauled away, Quincy howled, "This won't stand! This won't stand!"

RUSTY NAIL SALOON, BANE, NEVADA

Looking down the bar in either direction, Isaac found himself surrounded by men in his similar state of mind: distraught, tired and defeated. It made sense; who else would drink this early in the morning?

"One more," Isaac said, waving to the bartender.

The bartender placed a full bottle in front of him and said, "I think you need the entire bottle."

Isaac nodded, pulled the cork, and filled his glass. Staring at the silky brown liquor, he began to doubt his decision. Not the one to arrest Wilkes but giving up the silver.

"This is what riches to rags looks like," Connor said,

walking up next to Isaac.

Surprised to see him, Isaac said, "I think I made a mistake."

"I tried to tell ya, but you're so damn righteous. Hell, you still haven't admitted you've been in prison though I know you have. You let your pride dictate this decision, and look at where we are now."

"I'm sorry."

"What are you doing in here anyhow? Shouldn't you be arresting people?" Connor said, pouring himself a glass from Isaac's bottle.

"I was fired. I'm no longer sheriff," Isaac replied then tossed the shot glass back, drinking the whiskey in one gulp. Wiping his mouth, he continued, "I miscalculated."

"You call it that; I call it leading with your emotions. You're too driven by those damn feelings, and now you have nothing. No girl, no silver, no badge, nothing except your damn emotions."

"I have a conscience. Should I just toss it aside?"

"Yes, you should. Do you honestly think Mr. Rich Man who lives in that big house on the hill will go bankrupt without his silver? Hell no. To him that was mere pennies. You forget, he owns this entire town. He could afford to lose that silver, it doesn't truly affect his life, while that silver would have set us up for our lives."

"I never told you what happened to me," Isaac said.

"I'm all ears," Connor said, drawing close to him.

"I don't know how you have this insight, but you do, you somehow knew I was locked up for something I didn't do."

Connor tapped his temple with his index finger and said, "I may not look smart, but I am."

"It was Lucy's father who did it. He objected to our engagement, and after an argument one evening, I went home. Along the way I witnessed a store being robbed. These poor people were merely trying to get coal so they could keep their families warm during the bitter cold. I saw a child in need, went to help, and somehow this was misinterpreted. I was knocked out in an altercation shortly after. I awoke in jail. From there I was rushed through what could only be described as a kangaroo court, then taken to prison. My sentence was twenty years. Can you believe that? Twenty years for something I hadn't done." Isaac groaned.

"My friend, you did do something, you stood up against the power brokers, the men like Mortimer Corrigan who think they own everything. The men who use us to get richer. Mortimer is no different than Lucy's father. You meant nothing to him; you were merely a pawn. Look at ya, you bring him his silver and how does he thank you? He tosses you aside like garbage," Connor said, taking the bottle and pouring them both drinks. "We're nothing to these people. We're just instruments to be used to enrich themselves."

"I never thought of it that way," Isaac said.

"That's because you were one of them at one time," Connor said.

"No, I wasn't," Isaac countered, not wanting to be included in that group.

"You went to college. You were no doubt raised in a nice house. I'm sure you didn't want for nothing. Am I right?" Connor asked.

"We weren't rich, but we weren't poor," Isaac said.

"Only rich folks go to college. Education is a luxury for those with means," Connor declared before drinking his shot.

"I'm not one of them," Isaac said.

"If you're not, then who are you?" Connor asked.

"I'm my own man. I have followed the law my entire life. I have fought for my country when she needed me, ready to sacrifice myself if need be," Isaac replied.

"And how many Mortimers went to fight? Huh? I say few. They remained behind and became richer; they exploited the war for their own greed," Connor preached.

Isaac let that sink in. There was truth to what Connor was saying, though he did know some sons of the wealthy went to fight and some died, so Connor's statement wasn't one hundred percent accurate.

"You're your own man, that is true, but a poor one with no future," Connor said. "Have you ever heard of Robin Hood and his Merry Men?"

"I have. It's an old English folktale, isn't it?" Isaac asked.

"It's about a man, a warrior, who loves his king, but a cowardly man, the sheriff who kneels to an evil prince, steals all that is his. Robin Hood fights to get what is his returned. His resistance inspires others to stand up for themselves, and quickly they form a merry band of outlaws who steal from the rich and give to the poor,"

Connor said, his mind drifting back to the days he was told the story as a young child.

"Are you saying I should be Robin Hood?" Isaac asked.

"Friend, you could never be as illustrious as Robin Hood. No, what I'm telling you is to stand up for yourself; take back what has been stolen from you. I can tell you're a good man. That silver, you would have used it for good. You would have taken it and enriched others' lives, the opposite of what Corrigan will do with it," Connor said.

Putting his drink to his lips, Isaac thought about everything Connor was conveying to him. It all made sense. He had played the game of life according to the rules he was told to play by, while he looked around and saw those who had status and success play by a different set. What did that get him? Yes, he could proclaim he was righteous, but on whose ears would that fall with a welcoming tone? He had fought in a war to maintain the republic and union. What he got in return was scars. He had worked hard to find solid employment as a lawyer in New York but kept bumping up against the nepotism of the elites. He had tried to marry the woman he loved, but his pedigree wasn't sufficient, so he was cast aside and jailed. He had fulfilled what was promised to Mortimer, and for that he was discharged from service. Connor was right, he had been nothing but a pawn his entire life, subject to those in power who played by their own set of rules and who would never allow him or others like him to advance unless they gave him permission. Now clear about his purpose, he turned to Connor and said, "You're the wisest man I've ever encountered in my life."

"You're making me blush." Connor smiled.

"Do you want to make some money?" Isaac asked.

"Not this again," Connor mused.

Taking Connor by the arm, Isaac squeezed gently and said, "We're going to take that silver back."

SHERIFF'S OFFICE, BANE, NEVADA

The second Mortimer set his eyes upon the somber-looking Quincy sitting behind bars, he felt more upbeat than having the silver found. Finally he had the man he hated right where he wanted, and it would be accepted in town that it was a just arrest.

"You won't win," Quincy spat.

"I got you red-handed. You were working with my aide to steal my silver so that you could open your own mining operation on that land to the south," Mortimer said, pacing back and forth, his hands clasped behind his back.

"Lies, all lies," Quincy shouted.

"You shut your mouth," Wallace barked from his desk.

"I won't shut my mouth, I won't. This is all a sham and I'll prove it in court," Quincy declared.

"I'm afraid it won't go so well for you. The thing is I run this town, I make its laws, and the court system in Bane isn't like other towns," Mortimer said.

"You still have to abide by the laws of Nevada, the

United States; I'm afforded my due process," Quincy snapped as he got to his feet and made for the bars. He thrust his arm through and attempted to grab Mortimer.

Laughing, Mortimer said, "You're not going to win this time. Your days are numbered, and a lowlife like you will pay for what he's done."

"This won't stand. You have no evidence," Quincy said, hedging that there was nothing on him, as he was a very careful person in his dealings.

Mortimer stood just outside Quincy's arm length and said, "You thought you could outfox me, that you were smarter than me. I went to Harvard; I studied economics and business. I've prepared my entire life to run companies, and you somehow thought that you, an uneducated wretch, would do me in. I'll have to admit that I was concerned for a period of time, but what I have that you don't is humility—"

Quincy laughed.

"It's true. Where I don't excel, I hire to fill that void. You see, Mr. Wilkes, I'm not like you, thinking you know it all; that hubris is your undoing. I surround myself with capable people, I don't keep them by threats or intimidation like yourself. I know your ways and they've met their match."

"So where is this sheriff you hired? How come he didn't arrest me?" Quincy mocked.

"Sheriff Travis served his part. He found the silver you stole and killed your man Marcus, but not before he told us your role in all of this…"

"Lies, all lies, I don't have the silver," Quincy fired

back.

"Sheriff Travis found your man Marcus with it at the livery. That's where your man died, protecting the silver you stole from me," Mortimer said.

"That can't be true, it can't be," Quincy blared.

"Oh, it is, and we have witnesses to the fact. More than Sheriff Travis, we have the McCarthy brothers; they both witnessed the events," Mortimer said.

As Mortimer's words sank deeper, Quincy realized that the one truth to all of this was that Marcus must have lied. If the silver had been recovered, it meant he'd been betrayed and his dream was unraveling.

"When I get out of here, I'll…" Quincy threatened.

"You'll do nothing," Mortimer said then turned to Wallace. "Take him to see the magistrate."

"Yes, Mr. Corrigan," Wallace said.

CHAPTER NINE

NOVEMBER 2, 1869

CORRIGAN RESIDENCE, BANE, NEVADA

Lucy didn't know how to ask Mortimer about what had happened to Isaac without fear of her concern drawing unwanted attention. All night she had lain awake, running through the different ways to address it. Upon his return the night before, he had simply mentioned that he wasn't coming back and that he'd been let go. Nothing more. She'd asked why, and he gave his typical Mortimer answer, which was simply, *He did his part.*

When Mortimer rose for the day, she got up with him.

As he got dressed, she found herself in front of the vanity, brushing her long brown hair. "Mortimer, I thought you liked the sheriff."

Lifting his suspenders, Mortimer replied, "He seems like a decent man."

"But I thought you liked him," she again said.

"I do."

"Then why let him go?" she asked.

"I told you, he did his part; time for him to move on," Mortimer answered, looking at his reflection in the long mirror, which hung on the wall.

She turned and asked, "All you could do was count

the days until his arrival. You had him stay in our house, doted on him, made him feel at home, then let him go. Don't you think he could have continued to do good work for us?"

"Why are you taking such an interest in the sheriff?" he asked, spying her glance in the mirror.

"You put a lot into him being here, and within days he's gone?"

He sighed, turned and said, "Since you insist on knowing, here's what happened yesterday. After finding my silver, I ordered him to arrest Mr. Wilkes, to which his reply was no. I again politely and professionally asked him to take Wilkes in for the robbery of the silver and the murder of eight people, but again the sheriff refused. So if he can't take orders from his employer, I don't need his services anymore."

"Why didn't he want to arrest Wilkes?" she asked.

"On account he said there was no hard evidence he had taken the silver or murdered those people. He kept insisting that he needed to find more evidence."

Hearing his answer, Lucy knew exactly why Isaac did what he did.

"Does that answer your question?" Mortimer asked, walking over to her and taking her hands in his.

"Has he left town?" she asked.

"I believe so. He came by and collected his pay and bonus, didn't say a word to me, then left. Last I saw him, he was riding west out of town towards the pass," Mortimer replied.

"He left?" Lucy said, her tone melancholy.

"You look sad," Mortimer said.

"I quite enjoyed having someone here. Our dinner the other night was a joy…"

"Until he got ill, poor fella. I don't know what to make of that," Mortimer said, going to the wardrobe and pulling out his suit coat. He slid it on, adjusted his tie, and continued, "Your father will be arriving tomorrow; best we have the room for him."

Lucy was lost in thought.

"Lucy my dear?" Mortimer asked before snapping his fingers.

Her head shot up. "Oh, yes, Father; it will be good to spend time with him."

"You don't look well. Have you taken your medicine yet?" he asked.

"I pray Sheriff Travis safe travels," she said.

"I do too, and I'm thankful he was here. I only wish he could have worked out for the long term; but the second he showed me he was incapable of obeying orders, he had to go. I know you understand. We must forever be obedient to those in charge," he said with a thin smile stretched across his face.

"Will you be home for dinner?" she asked.

"Not sure, I'm preparing for some meetings with some businessmen from San Francisco tonight," Mortimer replied.

"Who?" she asked, unsure whom he was referring to.

"Oh, there are these four businessmen in from San Francisco. They were working with Wilkes, but with his situation, we're now having discussions."

"That's good, dear," she said, not caring about his business life.

He gave her a peck on the forehead and left the bedroom. "Have a nice day."

"Bye," she said.

When the door closed, she lowered her head in despair. She hadn't lied to Isaac, she did miss him and even loved him, but she could never leave Mortimer, ever. She couldn't lie to herself that seeing him posed a dilemma, as she had considered running off with Isaac. What stopped her was the reality that Mortimer and her father would never stop looking, that they'd leverage their vast fortunes to bring her back. She might enjoy weeks, maybe even months with Isaac, but it would end, and when she would be dragged back to her life in Bane, it would be even worse than what it was now, and the consequences for Isaac would be harsh.

This was her life now, and she would just have to accept it.

SHERIFF'S OFFICE, BANE, NEVADA

Any plan to retake the silver couldn't happen if Isaac and Connor didn't know where it was. Armed with a hope and a prayer, Isaac walked into the sheriff's office, hoping one of the new deputies would help.

Isaac opened the door and cast a quick look inside. A swift wind whipped by him, chilling everyone present.

"Close the door if you're staying. Hell, just close the darn door," Jess hollered.

Isaac walked in and slammed the door. "Morning, gents."

"Hi, Sheriff," Porter said, waving.

"He's not the sheriff, stupid," Jess barked then gave an apologetic look to Isaac. "Sorry, but you ain't."

"I understand, no hard feelings," Isaac said. "Where's Sheriff Wallace?"

"He's out getting the silver you found secured before it gets shipped out to Carson City," Porter replied. He leaned over and spit into a spittoon.

"I need to see him; it's very important, critical really. Tell me where he is, and I'll just go to him," Isaac asked.

Jess cocked his head and said, "Whatever you got, we can relay it to the sheriff."

"It's sort of personal," Isaac said.

"Oh, c'mon, Jess, don't be so hard on Sheriff Travis. He done good when he was here," Porter said.

"He done got fired in record time. No, if he wants Sheriff Wallace, he can give us the message or he can wait."

Porter and Jess began to bicker back and forth.

"Never mind, I'll come back later. I just know he'll be disappointed he didn't know about it before then," Isaac said as he turned around to leave.

"He's over at shaft number two. That's where we're storing the silver until we ship it out the day after tomorrow," Porter barked.

"You're a damn idiot, Porter, you know that, a real simpleminded fool," Jess hollered.

Isaac tipped his hat and said, "Thank you and I

promise I won't do anything, Jess. If I had wanted to do anything, I wouldn't have turned in the silver in the first place."

"Whatever, you damn Johnny Reb," Jess growled.

Isaac shook his head and exited, having obtained the information he was looking for. Now the next thing he needed to do was scout out shaft number two.

***

Connor was waiting for Isaac on the corner. Upon seeing him exit the sheriff's office, he whistled.

Isaac came over and said, "Shaft number two."

"I know where that is," Connor said.

"The question is, how many people are guarding it?"

Stopping Isaac, Connor asked, "How prepared are you to get this silver? Are you willing to kill anyone?"

"No, I'm not."

"You should have told me that before you asked me again to get rich with ya. I don't know how we can steal heavily guarded silver without firing a shot," Connor said.

"There's always more than one way to do something," Isaac said.

"I can't wait to hear this plan." Connor laughed.

"Diversion, my friend, cause a big huge diversion," Isaac said with a broad smile.

"And what sort of diversion were you thinking?"

"I'll give you a hint, it starts with the letter *B*," Isaac said.

"Breasts!" Connor joked.

Isaac laughed out loud and said, "Hmm, that's an interesting idea."

"Oh, dear heavenly Father, please, oh, please make this plan involve breasts," Connor joked, clasping his hands together as he craned his head towards the sky.

"I said that was an interesting idea, but I was thinking of a diversion that goes…boom!"

"Explosives, I like that too," Connor said. "It's too bad that Wallace didn't let me stay on. Many of these details could be worked out."

"It makes sense, with Wilkes out of the way, there's no need for such a large number of deputies, and it was well known you were my hire."

Stopping in the street, Connor again looked to the sky and said, "I pray to Thee, please let us get this silver. If you grant me this prayer, Lord, I'll be a righteous son of God until I take my last breath."

"Do you always mock God?" Isaac asked.

"I'm not mocking God at all. I'm serious as I can be. If I get that silver, I'll change, I swear it. I'll be a different man," Connor said.

"Don't you see how silly it is praying that we'll be successful violating one of his commandments?" Isaac said.

"Oh no, I don't believe the Lord finds this silly, and I do believe in my heart that taking from these rich bastards is a Godly thing," Connor said.

Shaking his head in disbelief, Isaac said, "Enough talk. Let's go find where we can get some explosives."

"That's easy."

Furrowing his brow, Isaac asked, "It is?"

"They just keep it in a barn near the shafts. No one guards or watches over it. We can just sneak in their tonight and get a crate."

"TNT?"

"Yep."

"Well then, we just need to figure out what we're going to blow up tomorrow night," Isaac said.

CHAPTER TEN

NOVEMBER 3, 1869

CORRIGAN RESIDENCE, BANE, NEVADA

Mortimer kept pacing back and forth in the parlor, stopping every minute to look out the front window.

"Would you please stop doing that," Lucy said, growing agitated by his clear anxiety.

"I'm sorry, I'm just very nervous. Your father makes me very, very nervous," Mortimer said.

She laughed and said, "You're nervous about making your presentation, not about seeing him. Let's be clear."

She was right, Mortimer had never displayed this sort of anxiety before, so it had to be stemming from the proposal he was going to offer Everett.

Everett's reputation preceded him. Anywhere he went in New York, people knew his name and gave him respect. He was a likeable enough man, but it was a well-known fact that if you ever crossed him or provided inadequate service, you'd hear about it. If one ever sought to challenge him, then Everett would fight until he was sure you were crushed. Isaac knew that behavior better than anyone.

Seeing the coach making its way up the steep drive, Mortimer cried out, "He's here, he's here."

Again, Lucy laughed. "You're more excited to see my

father than I am."

"Oh shush," he said to Lucy. He raced out of the parlor and to the front door. "Phyllis, make sure you have a pot boiled for tea. I'm sure he'll want some."

"I will have it, sir," she called out from the kitchen.

Checking his reflection in the mirror to ensure he looked presentable, Mortimer practiced saying hello.

"Mortimer, please stop. You look silly," Lucy said, walking up to him.

"I need this to work," Mortimer said to her, the stress written all over his face.

She turned him so he faced her. Patting him tenderly on his chest, she said, "My father appreciates and respects power and confidence. How you're acting now will not help you. Be strong, respectful and clear in your delivery. Let the mining operation sell itself. You'll be fine."

"You sure?"

"I know my father. He likes you; believe me when I say if he didn't, we wouldn't be married," Lucy said.

The sound of the coach stopping sounded from out front.

"He's here," Mortimer said. Taking her hand, he opened the door and stepped out into the chilly late morning air.

The coach door opened and out came Everett. He was bundled up with a thick wool blanket wrapped over his shoulders. He glanced up at Mortimer and Lucy and said, "I thought the desert was supposed to be hot."

"How do you do, Everett? So good to see you," Mortimer said, racing down the stairs, arm extended.

Everett took his hand and shook it. "Nice to see you, Mortimer." He spun around and looked down on the town. "So this is Bane?"

Stepping up alongside him, Mortimer said, "That's it, that's my town."

"Your town, hmm," Everett mused.

"When do you think you'll—" Mortimer said before being interrupted.

"Hello, Father!" Lucy cried out.

Everett turned and waved. "Lucy, you look well." He walked up the steps and embraced her. "It appears Mortimer is not feeding you well enough; you're skin and bones."

"Well, she's been ill much of the time since we've been in Bane," Mortimer said defensively.

Everett ignored Mortimer and continued, "Is he taking care of you?"

"He is," she answered.

"Come inside," Mortimer said, walking past them and opening the door.

Everett and Lucy stepped over the threshold and entered the house.

Removing the blanket and his overcoat, Everett stretched and sniffed loudly. "What's that I smell?"

"That would be your favorite, Father," Lucy said.

"Roast pork, and are you serving it with macaroni?" he asked, his eyes wide with excitement.

"Macaroni with parmesan cheese, Father, just how you like it," Lucy said happily. It made her feel good knowing he was content.

"When is supper served?"

"Four o'clock," Mortimer said.

"That's a bit early for me, but I'm so hungry, that will be sufficient," Everett said.

"Would you care to get washed up?" Mortimer asked.

"Yes, that would do, that would do nicely," he answered.

Lucy showed him the back bedroom, the same one Isaac had used during the time he'd spent there.

Returning to the parlor, Mortimer asked her the second she walked in, "Is he in a good mood? He seems to be."

"He seems himself, but happier," Lucy answered.

"Oh, you don't know how that makes me feel," he said, hugging her firmly.

"Oooh, you seem pleased as well." Lucy chuckled.

"I am, dear, I am," Mortimer said. He went to the liquor cart, opened the brandy decanter, and poured himself a glass. "Care for a brandy?"

"Yes, I'll have one, thank you," she said.

Heavy footfalls sounded in the hallway.

"Here he comes. Do you think he'll want brandy or tea?" Mortimer asked.

Everett appeared in the doorway, his face flushed red. He held up a piece of paper and growled, "What is the meaning of this?"

Looking bewildered, Mortimer asked, "Meaning of what?"

"I'm talking to you, daughter. What is this?" Everett

asked, waving the paper in her direction.

Knowing full well what he had in his hand, she answered, "I told him he needed to leave, but he wouldn't. He's gone now though."

"I'm confused. Are we talking about Sheriff Travis?" Mortimer asked.

"Your wife's former beau was here in your house and you didn't know?" Everett asked Mortimer, his nostrils flared with anger.

Confused, Mortimer said, "Former beau, um, there must be some misunderstanding. The last person to stay in that room was Sheriff Ethan Travis."

Everett marched over to Mortimer and handed him the note. "Read it."

"Mortimer, it's not what you think. Nothing happened. I told him to leave, I told him," Lucy said, her tone displaying the sadness in her heart.

Mortimer read the note, his eyes growing wider as they passed over more and more words. When he was done, he lowered the note slowly and looked at her; his eyes showing the pain he was feeling. "Lucy, who's Isaac?"

"He was her former beau. The son of a bitch tried to marry her, but he was convicted of robbery and conspiracy and sent to prison. He's supposed to still be there, but apparently he's not," Everett explained.

"Was this Isaac here at the house? When?" Mortimer asked.

Fanning herself, Lucy quickly took a seat on the couch, feeling faint. "Let me explain."

"Don't explain this away! Was this man in our house?" Mortimer roared.

"Yes, yes, he was," she answered.

"We need to organize a search party immediately. He's an escaped convict; he's a very dangerous man," Everett said.

"When, when was he here?" Mortimer asked.

"He was here for three nights," Lucy replied.

"I don't understand. How is that possible? Sheriff Travis was here? Was he hiding in the house somewhere?" Mortimer asked, still not putting two and two together.

"Does it matter, Mortimer? Get your police on this immediately," Everett barked.

"Everett, please give me a moment with my wife!" Mortimer shouted.

Not one to allow anyone to raise their voice to him, Everett forgave Mortimer this time due to the circumstances. He backed away and went to stand near the fireplace.

"Lucy, I need you to be very clear and tell me everything right this very second," Mortimer said, sitting down next to her.

"Isaac arrived on October 29 and left the house on November 1. He spent three nights here," Lucy answered.

"That doesn't make sense. Where was he hiding?" Mortimer asked.

"In the back room, he stayed in the back bedroom," Lucy said.

"How is that even possible? Sheriff Travis was staying in that room," Mortimer said.

"Mortimer, don't you see, Isaac is Sheriff Travis," she confessed.

Mortimer's face turned ashen and his eyes bulged. "I-I don't, how is, when..." he stuttered. Mortimer's thoughts were jumbled, and he was finding it hard to concentrate.

"Isaac Grant, my former fiancé—" Lucy said before being interrupted by Everett.

"He was never your fiancé because you were never officially engaged," Everett blurted out.

"You're telling me the man who said he was Sheriff Travis was your old fiancé? The man who was arrested and put in prison four years ago?" Mortimer asked.

"Yes," Lucy said.

"You're telling me I had a convict, your old fiancé, under my roof, eating my food, drinking my—"

"Yes, I don't know how he knew to assume that man's identity or if there ever really was a Sheriff Travis; but that man who was here for three nights was not Sheriff Travis, he was most definitely Isaac Grant," Lucy confirmed.

Mortimer jumped to his feet and raced for the door.

"Are you going to inform your police?" Everett asked.

"I'll be back shortly," Mortimer said, grabbing his coat and hat.

"I wish to come," Everett said, racing past Lucy to meet Mortimer at the door. "We need to catch this escaped convict and hang him from the nearest tree."

"He'll be dead before a noose ever found its way around his neck because I'm going to kill him with my bare hands," Mortimer growled. He opened the drawer of the table in the foyer and removed an 1860 Navy Colt. He shoved it in his waistband, opened the door, and exited the house.

Everett was right behind him.

When the door closed, Lucy began to sob uncontrollably.

Phyllis went to her side and began to console her. "I know it might seem you're in a heap of trouble, but times like this come and go. Just know that I'm here for you."

"What have I done?" she sobbed.

"You've done nothing wrong, ma'am. That man of yours, the old fiancé, it's his fault; he came here."

"I don't know what I'll do," Lucy cried.

"Come here, cry on my shoulder," Phyllis said.

***

Outside, Mortimer didn't bother to go to his barn to get horses. By the time he'd have them saddled, he would already be sitting in front of Wallace.

Trailing just behind him, Everett pounded away on the point that Isaac must be caught and how he was a very dangerous man.

"We'll catch him, Everett, that I can assure you, and when we do, I promise you, I'll kill him."

SHERIFF'S OFFICE, BANE, NEVADA

"I don't give a damn. Pull everyone you have, everyone! I want him found!" Mortimer yelled, his voice cracking.

Wallace nodded and said, "I'll get everyone on it, sir."

"I mean everyone. Pull every deputy you have; put out a reward, I don't care. I want him found, and I want him in that cell there by the end of the day," Mortimer howled.

Overhearing the commotion, Quincy shouted, "Ha, your sheriff was a wanted man? This is too rich."

"You shut your mouth, or I'll have one of my deputies put a bullet in you," Mortimer barked.

"The great Mortimer Corrigan hired an escaped convict to be the sheriff of Bane. Wait until word gets out about that," Quincy fired back.

Unable to control his temper, Mortimer pulled his pistol, cocked it, and walked up to the cell where Quincy was being held. "Keep your filthy mouth shut!" he screamed.

"Or what? You gonna shoot me? That's murder," Quincy shot back.

All eyes were on Mortimer and what he was going to do. While he was an even-tempered man, he didn't like to be challenged. He'd never escalate a situation to a fight; he would just find another way to get back at someone who crossed him. But that was how Mortimer normally handled things; today was not normal.

Everett approached and said, "Ease up, Mortimer.

You don't want to do something you can't take back."

"Listen to the old man." Quincy cackled.

"I'll…" Mortimer roared, his jaw pressed tightly closed. His entire body was tense, causing his right arm to shake as he held the Navy Colt, its muzzle pointed at Quincy's head.

"You won't do anything," Quincy again spat.

Mortimer's finger was on the trigger and applying pressure.

"Please, son, don't do this," Everett said.

Everyone in the room was frozen in anticipation of what Mortimer would do.

Taunting him, Quincy walked towards Mortimer and pressed his face against the bars, the muzzle now inches from his face. "Go ahead, shoot me in front of all of these witnesses."

"Sheriff Wallace, send everyone outside. Start looking for Isaac Grant, aka Sheriff Travis," Mortimer ordered.

"Right now, sir?" Wallace asked.

"Yes, right now!" Mortimer yelled.

Everett turned to the hovering group of deputies and said, "You know what he looks like. Now you heard Mortimer, start looking for him." He waved and pushed people towards the door.

Wallace remained, his gaze on the tense scene near the cell.

"Sure, get them to leave. If I'm found dead, they'll still know you did it," Quincy taunted.

"Sheriff, when is it legal to shoot a man?" Mortimer

asked.

Hearing the question, Everett did an about-face and came back. "What are you doing?"

"Everett, get away from me," Mortimer snapped. "What's the answer, Sheriff?"

"In self-defense or in the defense of others," Wallace answered.

"Open Wilkes' cell door and hand him a pistol," Mortimer ordered.

"This is not a good idea," Everett said.

"I agree, this is a very bad idea," Wallace said.

"Do I have to fire you too?" Mortimer asked.

Giving in to Mortimer's bloodlust, Wallace stepped up and said, "Mr. Corrigan, it's just us now. If you want to shoot him, I'll back up your story."

"You will?" Mortimer asked, giving him a quick glance.

"This is lunacy," Everett howled, finding it hard to believe he was about to witness his son-in-law murder an unarmed man.

After hearing what Wallace said, a look of fear washed across Quincy's face. "You're going to let him kill me in cold blood?"

"I can't be a part of this," Everett said and promptly left.

"It's just us now, Mr. Corrigan," Wallace said into Mortimer's ear.

Terror now gripped Quincy as he cowered in the corner. "You're the sheriff. You can't let him shoot me."

"Mr. Wilkes, watch me," Wallace said with a smile on

his face. "And do you know why I'm fine with this? Because you had my friends killed, you did. You don't deserve to be alive."

A devilish grin now stretched from ear to ear on Mortimer. He closed his left eye, aimed and squeezed the trigger. The .36-caliber round ball burst from the muzzle, striking Quincy in the face.

"Good shot," Wallace cheered.

Quincy toppled to the floor and began to crawl around. The round ball had entered just below his nose but didn't exit out the back of his skull. Thick, dark red blood poured from the gaping hole in his face.

"Open the cell," Mortimer said.

Wallace complied.

Mortimer entered, cocked the pistol, placed the muzzle against the top of Quincy's head, and pulled the trigger.

Quincy's body instantly went limp.

Mortimer shoved the pistol back into his waistband and said, "Thank you, Sheriff. I'll pay you a bonus for giving me the privilege of serving justice here today."

"Why, thank you, sir," Wallace said.

"Now shall we go find the old sheriff?" Mortimer asked.

MCCARTHY LIVERY AND STABLES, BANE, NEVADA

Duncan ran into the livery barn and slammed the door shut. He raced through, stopping at the last stall, where

Connor and Isaac sat chatting about how to execute their plan. "Hey, boys, I thought you should know that the law is looking for the sheriff there."

"Looking for me?" Isaac asked.

"I was just at the mercantile, and a couple of deputies came in. They asked around and said that you were wanted because you're an escaped convict and that you're not really a sheriff; that your name is Isaac Grant," Duncan explained. "Is that true?"

"It is true, so what are you going to do about it?" Connor asked his brother.

"If I had the intention of doing something, I wouldn't have come to warn ya," Duncan answered.

"What should we do?" Connor asked.

"I'm not leaving without the silver and without trying one more time to convince Lucy," Isaac said.

"Give it a break with the little lass." Connor sighed.

"I'll regret not going to see her again. I just need to confirm one last time," Isaac said.

"Boys, there's a good chance they'll come here looking for ya, and while I like ya, I don't want you gettin' me in trouble," Duncan said.

"You're throwing him out?" Connor asked.

"I am, little brother. I can't risk my business suffering," Duncan replied.

"Where will we go?" Connor asked.

"We?" Isaac said.

"I'm going with ya, well, as long as you're still trying to get the silver," Connor said.

"Now more than ever. If we can hide until just

before the sun sets, the second shift in the mine lets out. That will set hundreds of hungry and thirsty miners loose in town," Isaac said.

"Yes!" Connor countered. "We're gonna get that silver."

Isaac held out his hand.

Connor took it and they both shook.

"You're a good friend, Connor," Isaac said.

"I just want the silver, that's my motivation," Connor joked.

"You can hide in the dry storage. It's a good spot," Duncan said, taking them to the barn he used to store carriages and such.

"Where is it?" Connor asked, not seeing anything but dirt.

"I rarely go down in it, so it gets covered by dirt," Duncan said.

"Why are you helping us, brother? Connor asked.

"'Cause we're family. Now shut up and help me," Duncan said.

Under Duncan's direction, they moved several crates from a spot near the back. Grabbing a push broom, Duncan brushed away dirt until a rope cord appeared. He bent down, grasped it and pulled.

The earth cracked, but it wouldn't budge.

"Help," Duncan said, straining.

Connor and Isaac took hold and pulled.

Their combined effort was enough to lift the dirt-covered hatch. Underneath was a ladder that led into the darkness.

Loud banging came from the livery door, startling them. "We're with the sheriff," a deputy hollered.

"Go, get down there," Duncan said. "I'll let ya out just before the sun sets."

"Thank you," Isaac said.

"If something happens and I don't come back, go get the silver and head to a place called Devil's Fork, it's directly south of here. Take the narrow trail that's at the end of the silt mound. Head down that trail for about ten miles, you'll come to a fork. If you go right, the trail widens. If you go left, it narrows further and goes down a dangerous set of switchbacks. At the end is Devil's Fork," Duncan explained.

"Be safe," Isaac said then disappeared into the cellar.

Before Connor descended, Duncan grabbed him and said, "I'll meet you there in the morning, at first light, with a wagon."

"A wagon?" Connor asked.

"It's for our share."

"Will we not be traveling with him?" Connor asked, tilting his head in the direction of Isaac.

"I'm coming with ya, baby brother, but I don't want to journey with your friend past the Devil's Fork. I say we head to Mexico or maybe even Texas," Duncan said.

Tears wet Connor's eyes, knowing his brother was on his side. "Love you, brother."

Duncan lowered the heavy door, pushed dirt and hay over it, then set a few crates on top to help camouflage it.

The banging at the door continued.

"I'll be back, brother," Duncan said and raced to the livery door.

BANE, NEVADA

From building to building they searched for Isaac but couldn't find him. However, they did get credible information that he had been there up until an hour before searching. This meant that either he hadn't been found or was heading away. The one piece of information that also came in was that Isaac had been seen with Connor, making Duncan a suspect. He was now being held for questioning.

With nothing to show for their hours of searching, Mortimer gathered his men and the many volunteers hoping to get the hefty bounty placed on Isaac's head.

Looking at the fifty plus men gathered, Mortimer hollered, "We've searched the town, almost every square inch. We now must consider that he's fled the town and is out there!" He pointed out to the hills beyond. "We're going to get four teams together. One will head north, another south and so forth. I want every able-bodied man on this; pull them from everywhere. I only want to have a skeleton crew left here to walk the streets looking. Now Sheriff Wallace here will assemble the teams and, Sheriff, I mean everyone, pull everyone but a few bodies."

Wallace nodded then pulled Mortimer aside. "Mr. Corrigan, do you really mean everyone?"

"Yes, pull every able-bodied person. I don't want people standing around. Those who stay will be on watch in the streets."

"Everyone? Even security and guards at the mine?" Wallace asked, attempting to get clarification.

"Damn it, Sheriff, is English a second language for you? I said everyone. Finding Isaac Grant is this town's, your office's top priority," Mortimer barked.

Everett watched on, proud of Mortimer and the forceful approach he was taking.

"Yes, sir, I'll pull everyone for the search," Wallace said and ran off.

"You're doing a damn good job. You run this town very efficiently. I'm proud of you," Everett said, draping his arm over Mortimer's shoulder.

"That's nice of you to say. It's not been easy."

"You don't know this, but I'm a forgiving man. I'm strict, I also hold people accountable, but you're dealing with this strongly. I wouldn't have done what you did with that man in the cell, but like I said, I'm a forgiving man."

"That man was sabotaging this operation and had murdered eight men; half of them were deputies. He needed to suffer the consequences. This is my town, my laws."

"Like I said, you're handling this with strength. I'm impressed," Everett said, and he was serious. Though he personally wouldn't have killed Quincy, he might have had someone else do it. What impressed him the most with Mortimer was how he didn't mind getting his own hands dirty. He'd never seen Mortimer in this light, and it was refreshing to know his daughter was with a man of power and determination.

"Will you ride with me?" Mortimer asked Everett.

"It would be my honor," Everett answered.

"Then let's go ready the horses," Mortimer said.

MCCARTHY LIVERY AND STABLES, BANE, NEVADA

The sun was setting, yet Duncan hadn't returned.

"Where is he?" Isaac asked, concerned.

"I fear my brother is in trouble. I need to go find him," Connor said, pushing with all his might but barely budging the hatch.

"Let me help," Isaac said, getting on the ladder next to him and pushing with all his might.

The hatch lifted, but they could tell some crates were on top.

"The daft fool put heavy crates on it," Connor barked.

"Let's try again on the count of three—one, two, three," Isaac said.

The two used every ounce of strength they had and managed to get the hatch high enough that the crates slid off. They climbed out and lay on the floor, huffing and puffing.

A bell clanged in the distance.

"That's the second shift ending," Isaac said.

"That's great and all, but I need to go find Duncan," Connor said, getting to his feet.

Grabbing hold of his arm, Isaac said, "He told us to

go ahead and that he'd meet us at dawn. Let's go do this. Let's go get that silver."

Connor thought for a bit and said, "I know what my damn fool brother told us, but I'm going to go get him."

"You can't," Isaac said.

"But we can stop to go get your Lucy?" Connor asked.

"You're right. Let's go find him," Isaac said.

As they got to their feet, they heard the door creak open.

Looking up, they had nowhere to go, so left with no options other than fighting, Isaac grabbed a pickax handle and raised it.

In came Duncan out of breath. "Whoa, don't hit me with that."

"Where have you been?" Connor asked, embracing Duncan.

"I told ya I was coming back. I was just a wee bit late on account the sheriff wanted to question me. Apparently they're looking for you now too," Duncan explained.

"And he let you go?" Connor asked.

"Yeah, they've all left town, gathered four large posses to go ride, but—"

"How will we leave with the silver?" Connor asked, cutting Duncan off.

"If you let me finish, I'll tell ya," Duncan said, giving Connor an annoyed look. "I told them I'd seen ya and that I gave ya two horses and that ya were riding to Elko to catch the train. So many of the posse headed off in that direction. The second word got out that ya two were headed that way, their four posses dwindled down. Some did go in the other directions, but most went west. And get this, I was sitting in the sheriff's office and those deputies were arguing and bitter because they had been told to stay. Thing is, there's a large bounty on your head, Sheriff, and so as not to be left out, they just took off and left me sitting there. I came outside to find that even the men they'd told to stay had departed. It turned into a bit of chaos. Ya should have seen Mr. Corrigan yelling and screaming for order, but what I told them spread like wildfire."

"Brilliant," Connor yelped.

"That is good news," Isaac said.

"Oh, you like good news? I have even better news. They took everyone with them, and I mean everyone who could walk upright. That means they took the guards from the silver." Duncan chuckled.

"Well, can you believe it?" Connor asked.

"Too good to be true," Isaac said.

"It is true. That sheriff who took over for you is a real daft fella," Duncan said with a big smile.

"Come, gentlemen, let's go get that silver," Isaac said.

MINE NUMBER TWO STORAGE, BANE, NEVADA

Just as Duncan had described, the town, minus the miners letting out, was empty of any deputy or guard. They simply walked into the storage, and there sat the covered wagon.

"This just can't be. They left it unguarded," Isaac said, astonished by the development.

"What do you suppose got into Mr. Corrigan to allow this to happen?" Connor asked.

"Who knows, but let's not stand around talking. Hitch the horses to the wagon; let's pull it out," Duncan said, bringing two horses into the storage area.

With the wagon hitched, they drew it out of the storage.

Duncan had also brought his own wagon so they could split the silver between them.

Connor tossed open the flap and was greeted by the worst kind of odor. "What in the world?"

Isaac glanced in and saw the two bodies were still in there. "They didn't remove them."

"Let's hurry and dump them inside," Duncan said, about to climb on board.

"Who goes there?" a voice boomed from just outside the storage area.

The men froze.

The voice boomed again. "Who goes there?"

Isaac pulled his pistol from his holster and cocked it back.

Silence for a few moments was followed by a single crack of gunfire.

Duncan hit the ground and crawled away while Connor took cover behind the wagon. Isaac, though, was on a mission and wasn't going to be stopped. He stepped out, pointed his pistol and fired, cocked again and fired.

The stranger dropped to the ground with a thud.

Isaac ran over to find a deputy he'd hired lying dead on the ground. "Gentlemen, we need to go."

Hollering and yelling broke out in the distance.

"Now!" Isaac barked, running back to the wagon.

"We need to transfer our share to the other wagon," Duncan said.

"No, let's go," Isaac said.

Duncan got on his wagon and pulled away.

Connor got onto the covered wagon with the silver and took hold of the reins.

Isaac climbed onto the back of a horse, but instead of turning to head south, he pointed the horse back towards town.

"What are you doing? No. They've been alerted. Don't do this," Connor begged Isaac, knowing what he was about to go do.

"I have to try one more time," Isaac said.

"No, come with us," Connor said.

"I'll meet you at Devil's Fork. If I'm not there before dawn, head out."

"We'll wait for you," Connor said, slapping the reins hard against the backs of the horses.

Isaac kicked the ribs of his horse, causing it to rear and race towards town.

CORRIGAN RESIDENCE, BANE, NEVADA

When Isaac reached the house, his heart felt like it was about to explode. He didn't know what to expect but was prepared for anything. With his pistol in his hand, he approached the door and saw his things sitting next to it still. They'd not been touched since he was evicted from the house days ago. With little time, he banged on the door.

Phyllis opened up and said, "Sheriff Travis, or whoever you are, you're not wanted here." She attempted to shut the door, but Isaac stuck his boot across the threshold.

"I need to see Lucy," he said.

"That's not possible."

"Phyllis, step aside. I need to see her," Isaac demanded.

"Sheriff, I was given specific instructions not to allow you inside. Please be on your way," Phyllis said, her voice cracking with fear.

Impatient, Isaac pushed his way inside and called out, "Lucy! Lucy, where are you?"

"Sheriff Travis, I demand you leave this residence immediately," Phyllis barked.

Ignoring her, Isaac went farther into the house. "Lucy!"

Appearing at the top of the stairs, Lucy replied, "What are you doing here? You need to go, they're looking for you, and if they find you, they'll kill you."

"I'm here for you," Isaac said, running up the stairs to the landing. He holstered his pistol, took her hands, and said, "Come with me."

Phyllis cried out, "Sheriff Travis, leave Mrs. Corrigan alone and leave this house this instant or I'll get the shotgun!"

"Lucy, please, this is our moment; come away with me," Isaac begged.

"I can't, you know I can't. I thought I was clear in my note the other day," Lucy said, pulling away from him.

"I have the money, lots of it. We can run away together, go very far away, and make a real life for ourselves. We won't have to struggle. I know you wanted me to have means, and now I do, but I don't have time to waste, we must leave now!" Isaac insisted.

Sensing he'd done something wrong, she asked, "What have you done?"

Phyllis began to climb the stairs, a shotgun in her shaky grasp. "Sheriff Travis, you must leave Mrs. Corrigan alone and leave this residence now or I'll...I'll shoot you."

"You won't shoot me, Phyllis. You know I'm not a bad person," Isaac said. Putting his focus back on Lucy, he said, "I've only done what Mortimer or your father would have done. I took advantage of a situation for myself. I have more than enough to take care of us for the rest of our lives, but we can't stand here and think about it, there's no debating."

Shocked, Lucy took more steps away from him. "Did you steal something?"

"I took the silver shipment," Isaac said.

"You are a thief," she said, her mouth wide open in awe at his confession.

"Not any more a thief than your husband or your father," Isaac countered.

"They're businessmen; you're a common robber," she fired back.

"If you only knew what Mortimer did to even get this town, you'd call it stealing, or how your father lied to have me imprisoned. What else has he done?" Isaac said.

"You're lying. You're a liar and a thief. You're everything my father ever said you were," Lucy bellowed.

"That's not true," Isaac said defensively.

"Get out of here!" she yelled.

"But, Lucy, we love each other; we can now finally be together, as we planned years ago," he said, stepping towards her.

The closer he got, the farther she backed away from him.

"Leave. You're not the man I knew back then. He was honest, upright, a good man. You're a common thief and a liar. You showed up representing yourself as another man. Where is the real Sheriff Travis? Did you kill him? Did you kill him then take his identity?"

Isaac could see how it must have looked, but she wasn't aware enough to know how Mortimer or her father operated their businesses.

"Leave!" she screamed.

Finally seeing there was no hope convincing her and that any idea of them ever being together was gone for good, he retreated down the stairs. Just before leaving, he looked back over his shoulder to see her embracing Phyllis, her sobs echoing through the house. Knowing he was out of time, he exited the house, hopped on his horse, and rode away.

THREE MILES SOUTH OF BANE, NEVADA

Isaac rode as fast as the horse would take him on the narrow and rocky trail, his thoughts swamped by Lucy's cry for him to leave. It was the moment he'd been looking to have. He'd needed closure one way or the other, and it was now over. She'd made up her mind about him and their future. There wasn't a thing he'd ever be able to say to her to mend what had been shattered by lies four years before. He was saddened yet felt liberated. He'd come to Bane to get the answers he was looking for and was now leaving with them and a pile of silver, and, no, he didn't consider it theft, he considered the silver now payment for his wrongful incarceration.

So lost in thought he didn't hear the horses coming towards him until it was too late.

Almost running into a group of four men on horseback, Isaac pulled back on the reins, bringing his horse to a hard stop, which almost resulted in him being thrown. The sun's light was almost vacant from the sky, but there was enough for him to make out that it was Mortimer.

"You!" Mortimer howled, reaching for his pistol.

Isaac was faster, pulling his, cocking it with one hand, and firing. His round hit Mortimer in the shoulder. He spun off the horse and hit the ground.

Everett, who was next to him, raised his hands high and hollered, "Don't shoot."

The two deputies, Jess and Porter, who had also been riding with them, sat motionless.

Isaac cocked the pistol and pointed it at Everett. "I should gun you down right here for what you did to me."

"I only did what was eventually going to happen anyway. You're low-down scum," Everett spat.

Jess, sensing an opportunity, went for his pistol.

Seeing him move, Isaac pivoted in the saddle and pulled the trigger.

The round ball hit Jess squarely in the chest with a loud thud. He bent over backwards in the saddle and fell off the horse. He was dead before he hit the ground.

Isaac cocked the pistol again but suddenly and fearfully remembered his cylinder was empty after having used it since killing Marcus, but he'd never changed the cylinder or reloaded. Bluffing, he pointed the pistol at Porter and barked, "Take your pistol out and toss it on the ground." Turning to Everett, he said the same thing.

Both men did as they were told.

On the ground Mortimer stirred.

"You two, move on ahead. Get," Isaac ordered.

"I'll find you. I'll spare no expense," Everett said as he slowly passed Isaac.

Not allowing Everett to leave unharmed, Isaac pistol-whipped him in the face, leaving Everett with a bloody and broken nose. "That's for having me locked up."

"I will find you, I will," Everett said.

"Leave or I'll put you in the ground," Isaac said.

Everett moved on, followed by Porter.

When they were out of sight, Isaac dismounted and walked over to a moaning Mortimer. He knelt down and asked, "How bad is it?"

"I'll live just so I can hunt you down," Mortimer spat.

"Good, looks like you'll live," Isaac said. He picked up his Navy Colt and shoved it in his waistband then got Mortimer to his feet. After helping him onto the horse, he said, "Don't come looking for me. If you do, I'll come back and kill you all." It was a threat that he didn't mean to follow up on. All he wanted to do was leave and never see these people again.

"I will find you," Mortimer roared.

"Best you get that wound attended to," Isaac said and slapped his horse on the rear end. The horse ran off.

Isaac watched until he disappeared around the corner. He questioned his decision not to kill Mortimer or even Everett, but that wasn't the kind of man he was. He regretted having to kill the one deputy but chalked it up to self-defense. He could be called a thief, but he wasn't a murderer. He climbed on his horse and rode off.

DEVIL'S FORK, NEVADA

Connor stood up and cocked the hammer back on the Winchester rifle when he heard the footfalls of a horse coming his way. He placed the butt of the rifle in the pocket of his shoulder and raised it. The only light that aided him in seeing was the small fire he'd made to stay warm.

"Don't shoot, don't shoot!" Isaac hollered as he emerged from the darkness. He pulled back on the reins and brought his horse to a full stop. "Put it down. It's just me."

"I wasn't sure. I can't see a damn thing," Connor said. "Where's Lucy?"

Isaac climbed off his horse and walked it up to the wagon and tied it off. "She's not coming."

"What happened?" Connor asked.

Isaac turned around and said, "Remember when I told you and Travis I was coming to seek an answer to a question? Well, I got my answer."

"Sorry, my friend," Connor said, genuinely feeling sorry for Isaac.

"Better you know than not know, that's what I say," Duncan said.

"I'm disappointed, but I'm also content at the same time, if that makes any sense," Isaac said, walking to the fire to warm himself.

"How's that?" Connor asked.

"Not knowing is always harder than knowing," Isaac said.

"That's similar to what I said," Duncan said.

"That reminds me of a time when I was a young lad. Duncan, you'll remember this. I got real sick, and I was having all these bad thoughts about what could be wrong with me. When the doctor came to the house, he diagnosed me with something very minor. It was the not knowing that was worse," Connor said.

"What are we going to do with all this silver?" Isaac said, looking over his shoulder at the wagon.

"Sell it, of course," Connor replied.

"But where? Do you know people who buy silver?" Isaac asked.

"You'll find someone to buy it in San Francisco. Just ask around, it's that simple," Connor said.

"You're not coming with me?" Isaac asked the brothers.

"Sorry, friend, we're heading south to warmer climes. Thinking of going to Texas," Connor replied. "Any idea where you'll go?"

"I'm thinking Australia or maybe even the Orient," Isaac replied.

"Isn't Australia where they take criminals?" Duncan asked.

"Yes, fitting, isn't it?" Isaac laughed.

The three chuckled.

Under the light of the fire, they divided the silver. They knew Mortimer would be coming and with a larger posse.

"The sun will be up soon," Isaac said, looking east.

"I hate goodbyes, but it must be," Connor said, opening his arms wide for an inviting hug.

Isaac embraced him. "I can't thank you enough."

"We're rich, Sheriff, we're rich." Connor laughed.

"Let's go, Connor," Duncan said.

"And thank you too," Isaac said to Duncan.

"My pleasure," Duncan replied, tipping his hat.

Connor climbed onto their wagon, tore off his hat, and howled, "If you ever find your way to Texas, look me up."

Isaac watched as the two brothers rode south,

quickly disappearing over a small rise. He looked west across the valley and towards the Sierra Mountains. He had many miles to go before he got to San Francisco with most of it being the unknown, but for Isaac, that was just fine.

EPILOGUE

DECEMBER 1, 1869

NEW YORK, NEW YORK

Gerald hobbled down the snow-covered street. Each labored step he took compounded the pain in his leg. After working twelve hours, he was looking forward to sitting in front of his coal stove, eating a hot bowl of soup and the fresh bread he'd just purchased at the bakery down the street.

Arriving at his tenement building, he climbed the icy stairs carefully, ensuring he wouldn't slip and fall down. Making it to the top, he shuffled to the door and entered the building. Immediately he was welcome by a foul odor typical of this time of year. During the late fall and winter months, many of the tenants didn't use the outhouses out back due to the bitter cold. Instead, they'd urinate and defecate into bowls or pots, then leave them outside their doors, and they'd take them out to dump later.

This habit disgusted Gerald, though it was better than those lazy neighbors who merely dumped their waste out the windows and onto the sidewalks or alleyways.

He slowly ascended the stairs, taking each step with care.

Upon reaching his floor, he was greeted by Evan, the

ten-year-old boy who lived next door. "Mailman came to your apartment today."

"He did?" Gerald asked, surprised. He never received mail; in fact, the last time he'd received anything was when he was notified of his parents' deaths.

"He shoved it under the door," Evan said.

"Isn't this exciting," Gerald said with a smile. He unlocked his door, and there, as Evan had said, was an envelope. He picked it up and first noticed how thick it was. He looked at it closely but didn't find a return address. In the upper right-hand corner he saw a postmark for San Francisco and instantly guessed it was from Isaac. He threw a satchel he carried onto the table and set the letter on his chair next to the coal stove. Before he read it, he would get settled in for the evening.

After lighting his stove and changing into his nightclothes, he sat down and picked up the letter. Again he examined it, from the Lincoln and Washington stamps to the beautiful penmanship on the front. He marveled in the rare occurrence and wanted to savor it.

Now warm under the blanket draped over his shoulders, he took a knife and sliced open the top of the envelope. He removed the contents and set them on his lap. Unfolding the paper, he discovered inside was a wad of currency. He thumbed through it and saw it totaled five thousand dollars. Curious as to what the letter said, he read it. As his eyes glanced over the words, his heart filled with joy and gratitude.

Dearest Gerald,

Enclosed you will find the money I borrowed plus interest. I know you told me not to send it, but I did, as I felt was right. Without your help and friendship I wouldn't have been about to embark on a journey of a lifetime. I owe you so much and this small amount will never come close to repaying you.

I'll stay in touch.

Your friend.

P.S. Please do yourself a favor and go live life. Go back to Albany and enjoy the days and years you have left.

Tears formed in his eyes. Knowing Isaac was doing well and seemed happy gave him satisfaction beyond what words could express. He only wished he could write him back, but understood why he didn't include a return address.

Gerald read the letter several more times. Each time it brought tears. He looked at the stack of money and smiled. Isaac was right, staying in New York and slaving away at the docks wasn't a life suited for him. With what was left of his parents' estate and this money, he could go back to Albany and live comfortably.

With his plans set, he reclined in his chair, lifted a full glass of brandy high, and said, "Cheers to you, Isaac Grant. Safe travels."

SAN FRANCISCO, CALIFORNIA

Isaac looked at the ships moored along the wharf. Soon he'd be on one and headed west across the Pacific and towards a new life in Australia.

He didn't know what to expect, but knew his life in

America was over. He was drawn to the irony of going to Australia, a penal colony. He felt it was appropriate for him to live where other convicts were being settled.

Using some of the money he'd made from selling the silver, he secured new papers giving him the name of Isaiah Ethan Travers, a lawyer and sheriff seeking a fresh start after having lost his wife. The funny thing was a lot of Isaiah's backstory was true, minus the fact he was an escaped convict.

He was torn about the long trip, approximately nine weeks, having never spent more than a day on a ship in his life. To ease his anxieties about the trip, he'd purchased a stateroom on the ship to ensure his lodgings would be comfortable.

He walked down the dock until he reached the gangway for his ship and stopped.

Sailors and porters alike were rushing up with arms full of supplies loaded into crates. They'd promptly deposit them and race back down to grab another armful.

Seeing a man who looked important, Isaac strolled over. "I'm looking for Captain Hays."

The man removed a corncob pipe, gave Isaac a once-over, and said, "Who's looking for the captain?"

"Oh, sorry, I'm Isaiah Travers. I've booked a stateroom on the ship here."

"You have, have ya?" the man asked.

"Yes, now if you could point me in the direction of the captain, I'd like to report in," Isaac said.

"I'd be the captain of this fair ship," the man said.

"You're Captain Hays?" Isaac asked.

"Been captain of this here ship for almost five years. She's a good one too, never have had an issue with her, and she fancies the long voyages," Captain Hays said, removing the pipe from between his yellow-stained teeth.

"She's pretty," Isaac said.

"She's more than pretty, she's gorgeous. If I could marry her, I would," Hays said.

"When should I board?" Isaac asked.

"Follow me. I'll take you to your cabin," Hays said and sauntered off up the gangway. Every time he took a step with his right leg, he limped.

Noticing the limp, Isaac asked, "Are you injured?"

Stopping on the main deck, Hays turned and lifted his trousers to show a wooden leg. "Lost her during the war. A damn Confederate cannonball took her clean off from just below the knee."

"You fought in the war, so did I," Isaac said.

"Did ya now? You ain't no rebel, is ya?" Hays asked.

"No, sir, I fought with the Sixty-Fifth New York," Isaac replied.

"Good to know. Now follow me," Hays said.

The two darted around bustling sailors towards the aft of the ship. Once there, Hays opened a small door and said, "This is yours."

Isaac poked his head in and was astonished by how small it was. "Not too big."

"It's luxurious compared to where my crew sleeps," Hays said.

"You're right; thank you," Isaac said, tossing his bags on the cot. "When will we set sail?"

"In two hours. Settle in," Hays said. He turned and started to limp off. A thought popped in his mind; he turned back and said, "Mr. Travers, want to sit at my table for supper tonight? We can swap stories about the war."

"I'd like that," Isaac said.

"What do you do, Mr. Travers? What's your livelihood?" Hays asked.

"I'm a lawman; I've worked on both ends of it. I've been a sheriff and a lawyer," Isaac replied, happy to be able to tell the truth.

"I'll have my first mate summon you when it's time. Meanwhile, settle in and relax...and, Mr. Travers, don't get in my crew's way."

"Understood," Isaac said.

Hays marched off.

Not content with staying in his cabin, Isaac went topside to the quarter deck to avoid the hustle and bustle along the main deck. There he had a good vantage point of the harbor and other ships. Soon he'd be on the ocean and headed towards the unknown. He was content with not knowing the details because he had faith in the broader definition of life. He was an optimistic man at heart; he looked at the remaining years of his life as an opportunity for discovery. He knew he'd find work, find a place to live, and eventually find love again. The events in the middle of it would be filled with uncertainty, and that, he found thrilling. Many people needed certainty in life; he'd come to accept that life was going from one uncertainty to the next.

As he stared out across the glimmering bay, his heart filled with hope. He was now a truly free man. Free of the chains of physical imprisonment and free of the entanglements of his past. He could now chart his own course defined on his terms. He wasn't concerned about Mortimer or Everett finding him. The world was too big, and soon they'd fill their time with ways of enriching themselves even more. As he reflected on the past five weeks, he came to the final conclusion that it had all been a valuable lesson. It even could be defined as a blessing in some ways. Some wouldn't see it that way, but wasn't life about perspective? He couldn't control his past, it was what it was, so why waste energy on it? If he were to be successful moving forward, he decided to focus on what he could control, and that was the present.

With his newfound freedom Isaac pledged he'd wake each day with purpose and go about making it as good as it could be, because if anyone knew about how life could shift in an instant, it was him.

THE END

ABOUT THE AUTHOR

G. Michael Hopf is the best-selling author of THE NEW WORLD series and other novels. He spent two decades living a life of adventure before he settled down and became a novelist full time. He is a combat veteran of the Marine Corps and a former executive protection agent. He lives with his family in San Diego, CA

Please feel free to contact him at geoff@gmichaelhopf.com with any questions or comments.

www.gmichaelhopf.com

www.facebook.com/gmichaelhopf

G. MICHAEL HOPF

BOOKS by G. MICHAEL HOPF

THE NEW WORLD SERIES
THE END
THE LONG ROAD
SANCTUARY
THE LINE OF DEPARTURE
BLOOD, SWEAT & TEARS
THE RAZOR'S EDGE
THOSE WHO REMAIN

NEW WORLD SERIES SPIN OFFS
NEMESIS: INCEPTION
EXIT

THE WANDERER SERIES
VENGEANCE ROAD
BLOOD GOLD
TORN ALLEGIANCE

THE BOUNTY HUNTER SERIES
LAST RIDE
THE LOST ONES
PRAIRIE JUSTICE

ADDITIONAL BOOKS
HOPE (CO-AUTHORED WITH A. AMERICAN)
DAY OF RECKONING
DETOUR: A POST-APOCALYPTIC HORROR STORY
DRIVER 8: A POST-APOCALYPTIC NOVEL
THE DEATH TRILOGY (CO-AUTHORED WITH JOHN W. VANCE)

THE LAWMAN

Made in the USA
Lexington, KY
03 April 2019